READ ALL THE
SPY KIDS™
ADVENTURES!

COMING SOON!

SPY KIDS™

ADVENTURES

SUPERSTAR SPIES

Based on the characters
by Robert Rodriguez

Written by Elizabeth Lenhard

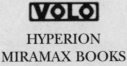

HYPERION
MIRAMAX BOOKS
New York

For information address Hyperion Paperbacks for Children,
114 Fifth Avenue, New York, New York 10011-5690.

Printed in the United States of America

First Edition

1 3 5 7 9 10 8 6 4 2

This book is set in 13/17 New Baskerville.

ISBN 0-7868-1805-0

Visit www.spykids.com

CHAPTER 1

Juni Cortez sat in his bedroom in front of his computer. He cackled fiendishly and rubbed his hands together in excitement. Juni couldn't have been happier. He was doing his favorite thing in the world—spying!

And he was good at it. After all, though he was only ten years old, Juni was a top spy with the OSS.

The OSS stands for the Office of Strategic Services. It's a top secret government agency with spies stationed all over the world. These highly trained spies can sense danger a mile away. Because of the OSS, evildoers are stopped before they can even *think* about doing evil. Plus, in their uniforms of cargo pants, utility vests, and combat boots, they look really cool!

As a Spy Kid, Juni had saved the world dozens of times. But today . . . he was spying for fun.

Giggling again, Juni opened a cardboard box and reread the note inside:

Dear Juni, the letter said. *Behold one of the slip-periest spying devices ever created. It's called the Eve's-Dropper. Isn't it cute?*

Juni fished the Eve's-Dropper out of the box. It looked an awful lot like a tiny garter snake—skinny, green, and shimmery. It had a pointed tail that whipped around, hitting Juni's wrist with a stinging slap. Its electronic eyes glowed red. Clutched in its miniature, silver fangs was a little red apple.

"I don't think I'd use the word *cute,*" Juni said skeptically. "But scarily smart—yes!"

Eagerly, Juni read on:

The Eve's-Dropper can slink into corners and slither into crannies. Every sound it encounters will be recorded— the apple is a microphone, you see. Simply align the Eve's-Dropper's bandwidth with your computer's audio input system and—Presto!—you've got instant intel, ready to send to OSS HQ for analysis.

Yours undercover, Uncle Machete

For a moment, Juni felt a little guilty. His uncle had created the Eve's-Dropper for fighting evil. That's what his Uncle Machete did, after all. He was the OSS's most brilliant gadget inventor. His ideas were always astounding, even if his execution could be, well, a bit dicey. Juni got queasy just *thinking* about Uncle Machete's Jumping Jack Flash, a rubber ball–shaped vehicle that *bounced* you to your destination. Or the disgusting Huffenpuff Hot-Air pills. Sure, they made you float, but they also tasted like melted crayons!

Still, there was one thing you could always say about Uncle Machete's inventions—they were made to fight evil and do good.

Juni, however, was planning to use the Eve's-Dropper for pure mischief—spying on his family. It was rascally and wrong. Juni paused for a moment.

Maybe I should do something worthwhile, he thought, like studying my spy manual or practicing the piano—something that would make my parents proud of me.

Juni gazed at the wily little Eve's-Dropper. Its red eyes looked back him. One of them seemed to wink!

Or . . . I could make Mom and Dad proud *tomorrow*, Juni declared to himself.

He unleashed another diabolical laugh. Then he set the Eve's-Dropper on the floor and began typing into his computer. In minutes, he'd mainlined the robotic snake's operational force into the hard drive. Next, Juni reached for his joystick and sent the Eve's-Dropper slithering out his bedroom door. The snake skimmed down the hallway of the Cortez family mansion.

Juni cocked an ear toward his computer and waited anxiously for some scintillating sounds.

The first thing he heard was the shuffling of papers and the scratching sound of a pen moving across paper. A rumbly voice with a silky Spanish accent echoed out of the computer speakers. It was Juni's Dad.

"Ingrid," Dad was saying to Juni's mom. "Do you realize our water bill went up twenty whole dollars this month? We have to be more conservative with our spending!"

"But, Gregorio," Juni heard his mom protest. As usual, her voice was lilting and light. "I used that extra water to fill up our Bermuda Triangle simulator. A spy can never train too much, you know."

That's right—Juni's parents were spies, too. In fact, a long time ago they'd been the most dangerous spies the world had even seen. But then they'd crossed each other's paths. They'd fallen in love, gotten married, and become parents—which isn't a very spylike thing to do. So, for a while, Mom and Dad had dropped out of the undercover business. They'd become humdrum computer consultants. They'd done ordinary things like driving school car pools and planning family vacations to Florida.

It was only when the OSS called Ingrid and Gregorio back for one last, irresistible, save-the-world mission that they'd returned to the spy game—without telling their family, of course.

The only problem with the scheme? Mom and Dad's spy skills had gotten a little rusty over the years. Soon into their mission, they'd been captured! That was when Juni had helped to rescue them—and become a spy himself!

Ever since that fateful mission, the Cortezes' lives as international superspies had been dramatic and action-packed.

Well, mostly. It seemed that nowadays, even international superspies had to do tedious things like pay the water bill.

Bo-ring, Juni thought with a yawn. He reached for the computer joystick and steered the snake out of his parents' bedroom.

Next, Juni heard a *whooooosh*ing sound. It was cascading water! Was it the Bermuda Triangle simulator sucking in some precious household object? A violent thunderstorm? Or maybe—

"You stick to me like gluuuuuuue*! And I dunno what to* dooooooo*!"*

Juni's older sister, Carmen, was singing country music in the shower!

"I'llllll love ya till the last cow mooooooos," Carmen sang.

Juni winced and clapped his hands over his ears. That is the worst song ever! he thought. What's more, Carmen's murdering it!

Luckily, when Juni lowered his hands, Carmen had moved on to a rock ballad—the latest chart-topper by superblond, superfamous pop star Daphne Lear.

"Saw him at the mall," Carmen warbled. Her voice echoed painfully off the bathroom tiles. *"He said he'd call, and that's not all."*

"Oh, man," Juni cried, chortling gleefully. "Wait'll the other Spy Kids hear thi—"

"Aiiiigggggh! Juni!"

Juni clapped his hands over his ears again. His sister's angry scream had blared out of the speakers very loudly; he was surprised his computer screen hadn't shattered.

Carmen's enraged outburst was followed by the *thump-thump-thump* of her bare feet in the hall-way.

And *that* was when Juni realized he'd forgotten one crucial fact when planning this devious mission—he was not the only Spy Kid in the Cortez house! Carmen was in the family biz, too!

And if there's one thing a spy should never do, it's spy on another spy.

Quick, Juni thought desperately. I gotta hide the evidence.

He reached for his computer's CD burner and popped out the fresh recording. He was just moving to stash the CD in a desk drawer when—

Slam!

"Juuuuuni!"

Juni froze in mid-stash. Then, stuffing the CD beneath his orange OSS shirt, he slowly turned to face the terrifying figure in his bedroom doorway.

It was Carmen, clad in a fuzzy, rainbow-striped bathrobe. Her dark, wavy hair was dripping water all over the hall carpet, and her chocolate-brown eyes were ablaze with fury!

Clutched in her fingers—still soapy from the shower—was a little green snake with an apple in its mouth.

Juni went pale.

Carmen took an angry step toward her brother and held up the Eve's-Dropper.

"To anyone else," she said, "this simply looks like a baby garter snake. Someone with truly excellent vision might notice the cute little apple in its mouth."

Carmen tossed the Eve's-Dropper onto Juni's bed.

"But a highly trained spy," she continued, "would notice that that particular apple has tiny holes in it. The same kind you would find in a microscopic *microphone!*"

Juni gasped. He'd totally been found out!

"Hand it over!" Carmen ordered, clenching her fists and advancing toward Juni.

"Hand . . . what over?" Juni squeaked. He rolled his computer chair backward.

"The recording you made of me singing in the shower, that's what," Carmen snapped.

"Uh . . ." Juni stuttered, "First of all, I don't know *what* you're talking about. And second—you didn't say the magic word."

"Which magic word would that be?" Carmen inquired. "'Please'? Or perhaps the magic word you were thinking of was . . . 'pummel'? Or 'pound'? 'Pelt with punishing blows' until you surrender?"

"Hey," Juni cried, leaping out of his chair in desperation. "That's more than one word!"

"A technicality!" Carmen yelled. She lunged at her brother. He sidestepped her and began to run across the room.

But Carmen wasn't going to let him go that easily. She leaped up high and began to whirl in midair. In fact, she whirled so fast the stripes on her bathrobe turned into a swirly cyclone of color.

Oh, no, Juni thought as he scurried across the room. I recognize that move. It's Spy Maneuver No. 125—the All-Day Sucker. And it looks like *I'm* the sucker! Pretty soon, Carmen's going to be smashing me with everything she's got.

Juni squeezed his eyes shut.

He hunkered down and braced himself for his sister's blow. In the last moment before Carmen completed her attack, he prayed for some sort of intervention.

Ah-whooo! Ah-whooo! Ah-whooo!

Wow, Juni thought, his eyes popping open. It worked! An alarm had begun blaring through the entire house, and a red light above Juni's bedroom door began flashing wildly.

Carmen halted in midwhirl and Juni straightened up. He shot his sister a taunting grin.

Before she could reply, the Spy Kids' mom called out from down the hall: "Stop everything you're doing, kids! That's the OSS alarm!"

CHAPTER 2

"**W**hoo-hoo!" Juni cried, darting out his bedroom. "I'm saved!"

"For the moment," Carmen yelled as she followed him. "Duty calls. But I haven't forgotten about that recording, Juni. You *will* be handing it over."

"Uh, sure, whatever," Juni said over his shoulder.

"Juuuni!" Carmen growled.

Before she could threaten her maddening little brother any further, the Spy Kids arrived at their parents' bedroom, where they sat themselves down in front of Mom's makeup mirror. Mom and Dad stood behind them.

"Ready?" Mom inquired.

"Ready!" answered Dad, Carmen, and Juni.

Mom reached over her kids' shoulders and tapped a few eye shadows and lipsticks lying on the vanity table. Or, to be more accurate, she pressed a few computer buttons made to *look* like eye shadows and lipsticks. Just a few keystrokes on those gadgets-in-disguise transformed the mirror into a giant computer screen. And on that screen was . . . a tricked-out rec room? Carpeted in green shag, the room was cluttered with lava lamps, video games, and smushy, lounge-ready furniture.

"Hey," Carmen said in confusion. "That's the VTVT set!"

"VTVT?" Dad said. "What is that? Some crazy new TV show?"

"A crazy TV *network*," Juni said, correcting his out-of-it pop. "It's Video Television Two. Carmen *loooooves* their star Vidjay, Rockin' Ralph."

"Shut! Up!" Carmen barked, turning bright pink.

Juni obliged his sister for one reason only— their boss, the head honcho of the OSS himself, had just come onto the screen. He was dressed in a tight, satin shirt and wore tiny sunglasses with blue lenses. His hair was slicked into youthful spikes. He spoke into a headset microphone.

"Wassup, wassup, Spy Kids?" he said.

"Uh . . . hi, Mr. Devlin," Carmen said. "I mean— er—wassup to you!?"

Devlin chuckled and slipped off his glasses.

"I thought this disguise was only appropriate to wear while giving you your next assignment," he said.

"Oh, uh, cool!" Juni replied respectfully. But furtively he turned to his sister and whispered, "Do you think our big cheese might have a little too much time on his hands?"

"Shhhh!" Carmen said, though she had to stifle a giggle as she said it. "Mission time."

"Carmen, Juni," Devlin said seriously. "I'm putting you on bodyguard duty."

"Bodyguarding!" Juni cried. He was unable to keep the intense disappointment out of his voice. "You don't need us to save the world? Or maybe a small country? A tiny island nation, even?"

"Nope," Devlin said cheerily. "Just one person."

"Oh," Carmen said. She was just as bummed as Juni. Bodyguarding was lame! "And, um, who would that special person be, Mr. Devlin?"

"Daphne Lear."

"Daphne Lear?" Carmen screamed. She began jumping up and down. "Daphne *Lear*? But she's a megastar."

"Uh-huh," Devlin confirmed, glancing at a printout in his hand. "She's won six VTVT music awards and eight Grimies *and* has come out with more than a dozen chart-topping pop songs."

"And she's gorgeous!" Carmen added excitedly.

"Yup," Devlin confirmed again. "She's made *Folks* magazine's Most Beautiful Stars list the past three years in a row."

"*And* she's sixteen and totally cool," Carmen said dreamily. "Maybe she'll teach me how to drive one of her seven cars. Or she'll give me some fashion tips!"

"Oh, no!" Dad suddenly sputtered. "I may not know about VTVT, but I know *all* about Daphne Lear. You'd have to be living in a cave not to. And I don't like the way that girl dresses."

"He has a point, honey," Mom said with a reluctant nod. "Like that bathing suit made entirely out of bubble-gum wrappers? Don't you think that was a little . . . much for a hospital ribbon-cutting?"

"*What*-ever!" Carmen said rolling her eyes. "All my friends and I *love* her."

"Don't feel bad, Mom," Juni said, patting her shoulder. "I don't really get the whole Daphne thing, either."

"I hope that won't impede your performance on this mission, Juni," Devlin said, speaking to him from the computer screen. "Because it will be starting any minute now. Miss Lear has a concert in your very city tonight. A stretch Hummer will be arriving to pick you up at approximately 0900 hours. After tonight's concert, you'll stay with Miss Lear for the duration of her four-week tour."

"A stretch Hummer!" Juni screamed. Now *he* began jumping up and down. "That's the coolest vehicle ever made—outside of Uncle Machete's workshop, that is. Wow! I *love* Daphne Lear."

" 'Tweens,' " Mom explained to her bewildered husband. "They're very fickle."

And pressed for time. Their departure time—0900 hours—was fast approaching. So, the moment they bid their boss adieu, the Spy Kids dashed to their bedrooms to pack for their mission.

Juni filled his spy bag with a bevy of high-tech gadgets, including the Eve's-Dropper Carmen had left on his bed. He also threw in a stash of snacks. At the last minute, he remembered to add some clean underwear and his toothbrush.

In her own room, Carmen tossed glittery make-up and lots of low-rise jeans into her spy bag. At the last minute, *she* remembered to add her laptop computer and some choice gizmos.

Soon, the Spy Kids were ready for deployment. And just in time! The moment they zipped up their bags, a horn began squawking from the driveway of their cliff-top manse. It sounded like a cross between a foghorn and a dying goose.

"That must be the Hummer!" Juni cried. He grabbed his spy bag and ran for the back stairs. "I've heard it's got the most macho horn in all of Autodom."

Landing in the kitchen, Juni bounced on the balls of his feet in excitement. His eyes bulged and his hands trembled slightly. When Carmen alighted in the kitchen, she glared at her brother in chagrin.

"Oh, man," she complained. "You're all geeked out. You're gonna totally embarrass me in front of Daphne Lear!"

"Will not!" Juni said.

"Will, too!" Carmen said.

"Not!"

"Too!"

"Snot!" Juni finally blurted out.

Carmen could not match her brother's grossness. She simply recoiled in disgust, while Juni giggled with triumph and delight.

"See, that's exactly my point," Carmen said. "You're way too uncool for this mission."

To this insult—this outrage!—Juni responded with the most effective riposte he knew.

"Mommmmm!"

"What is it, honey?" Mom cried, trotting down

the steps. She was carrying two duffel bags and wearing a look of alarm. Dad was right behind her.

"Carmen's calling me uncool," Juni whined.

Mom gave Carmen a scolding look, then turned to her son.

"Sweetie," she said. "That just isn't true. Weren't you just elected Most Courteous Spy Kid at the OSS? Courtesy is very cool!"

"Oh, puh-leeze," Carmen sighed.

"Speaking of 'too cool for school,'" Mom said, turning to wink at Carmen, "let's see what you've packed for your mission!"

Before Carmen could protest, Mom plucked her daughter's spy bag from her hand and un-zipped it. She raised an auburn eyebrow as a bunch of shiny, shimmery clothes spilled out onto the tiled kitchen floor.

"Just as I suspected," Mom said with a sigh. "Carmen, I know you want to impress Daphne Lear, but these clothes are completely impractical. How are you going to take down an intruder or dash Daphne to a getaway vehicle in these high-heeled shoes?"

"I'll . . . I'll manage," Carmen squeaked.

"Of course you will," Mom said, holding up one of her own duffels. "Especially since I packed you an alternative bag filled with *practical* cargo pants, spy vests, and athletic shoes."

"Ha-ha," Juni mocked, as Carmen's face fell.

"And, for you, mister," Mom said, tossing Juni the other bag. "A suitcase with a few less snacks and a few *more* pairs of clean underwear."

"Ha-*ha*!" Carmen teased, as Juni glowered.

But there was no time to bargain with Mom. (The kids would have lost, anyway.) The Hummer's horn was bellowing for them once again.

"Time to hit the road, my children," Dad said. "Four whole weeks on the road. Without us! I will miss you both terribly!"

He swept the Spy Kids up into a big good-bye hug. Mom kissed the kids' cheeks and slipped Juni a conciliatory chocolate bar.

As the kids headed out the door toward the waiting Hummer, Juni spotted Carmen furtively wiping a tear from the corner of her eye.

"Awwww," Juni cooed with mock concern. "Missing Mommy and Daddy already? How very cool!"

"Not another word!" Carmen gasped, turning toward Juni.

"Only if you never use the words *uncool* and *Juni* in the same sentence ever again," Juni offered.

Carmen huffed in indignation. Then she nodded. "Deal!"

Together Carmen and Juni approached the Hummer.

"Time to meet a real rock star!" Carmen declared.

CHAPTER 3

The Spy Kids hoisted themselves into Daphne Lear's Hummer. Then they blinked in surprise. The superlong SUV was *filled* with people. Half of them were chattering into cell phones. The other half seemed to be hidden behind glossy fashion magazines and handheld makeup mirrors.

"It's Daphne's entourage," Carmen whispered to Juni in awe.

"Her *what*-ourage?" Juni whispered back.

"You know," Carmen said, rolling her eyes. "The people who follow rock stars everywhere they go— managers, publicists, agents, high school friends, groupies. That's an entourage. I read in *Alpha Girl* magazine that Daphne's hangers-on are called Learjets. Y'know, because they're always flying after her, wherever she goes."

"*O*-kay," Juni whispered with a look of bewilderment. Then he shrugged and gave the other passengers a friendly wave.

"Hello, Learjets!" he called out cheerily. A couple of the members of the entourage looked at Juni with raised eyebrows. A few others scowled.

Carmen gasped softly and rolled her eyes.

"You don't call them that to their *faces*!" she hissed to her brother. "If I hadn't made a deal not to call you uncool, I'd be calling you uncool right now!"

Before Juni could reply, Carmen tried to do a little damage control.

"Uh, I'm Carmen Cortez," she said, introducing herself, even though nobody in the car seemed to be listening. "This is my brother, Juni. And we'll be guarding Miss Lear for the duration of the tour. And might I say what an honor it is to be aboard!"

"Right, right," blurted out a man with a thick British accent. He was wearing superskinny black pants and superbig, black-and-white shoes. His very bald head was very pale. A cell phone was plastered to his ear. And behind his black-framed glasses, his eyes were beady and bloodshot. "Tell us something we don't know. And would you kindly tell us after you've shut the car door? We're already running seven minutes late."

"Oh, now, Nigel," said a woman with big, blond hair and a thick Southern accent. She was sitting closer to the Spy Kids. "You be nice to these sweet little bodyguards."

The man merely gave Carmen and Juni a fishy stare as Carmen pulled the Hummer door shut. Immediately, the car began peeling down the Cortezes' driveway. The man resumed his agitated phone conversation.

"Oh, don't mind him," the Southern belle said to the Spy Kids. "He's Nigel W. Knot, Daphne's manager. He's just a little stressed out. He manages our crew and organizes the tour, the merchandising, the album sales, *and* all of Daphne's press interviews."

"Wow, being a rock star is serious business," Juni said, his eyes wide.

"I guess it is," the lady agreed, with a tinkly laugh. "I'm Ginny Jo Lear, by the way. I'm Daphne's mama!"

"Pleased to meet you, Mrs. Lear," Carmen said politely.

"Ginny Jo, please!" the lady said, patting her teased blond hair. "You'll make me feel like an old lady. Now, allow me to introduce y'all."

With a long, pink-painted fingernail, Ginny Jo began pointing one by one to the people hunched inside the extralong Hummer.

"Over there," she burbled, "we've got Dakota. She's Daphne's little sister, and we think she's got some real star potential, too!"

Dakota, who looked like a miniature replica of Daphne, shot the Spy Kids a sparkling, camera-ready smile.

"Then, we've got Kirstie and Christie," Ginny Jo went on, pointing at two giggly teenagers. "They're high school friends of Daphne's."

"See?" Carmen whispered to Juni.

"That fella over there is Daph's agent from IAB, which is short, of course, for the I Am Big talent agency," Ginny Jo continued. "And this is Daphne's publicist. And that's her assistant. And *that's* her assistant's assistant. Oh, and there's Charlotte! Charlotte, honey, I almost forgot you were here."

Ginny Jo was talking to a wan little woman squeezed into a corner of the backseat. She was so thin, pale, and mousy-haired she almost *was* invisible. She gave the Spy Kids a hesitant wave.

"This is Charlotte Bronstein," Ginny Jo explained. "Y'know, Daph's so busy we had to pull her out of her school in our hometown."

"Frog Woods, Alabama, right?" Carmen quickly piped up.

"My, but you've done your homework!" Ginny Jo cried, with another sparkling laugh.

"Well, with all due respect," Carmen said, "*everybody* knows the Daphne Lear story, even if they didn't see that made-for-TV movie about her on VTVT last month. She was just an ordinary girl from the southland until you brought her to an open audition for a variety show. She made the cast. And a couple of years later, Daphne made pop history when her first album went platinum only thirty-six hours after hitting the stands."

"That's right!" Ginny Jo cried. "And now I'm guessing you're wanting to meet the star herself?"

"She's here?" Carmen cried, looking around the crowded Hummer in surprise.

"Daph, darlin'," Ginny Jo said to a girl slumped behind a fashion magazine. The teenager's tanned, muscular legs were stretched out in front of her, making everybody else nearby scrunch up their legs to give her room. She was clicking her manicured nails impatiently on her armrest. Her diamond belly-button ring glinted harshly, and the red gem she wore on a gold chain around her neck was almost blinding in its brightness. (As any die-hard Daphne Lear fan could have confirmed, that ruby necklace was the star's signature bauble. She was *never* seen without it.)

"Daphne?" Ginny Jo said again.

A long-suffering sigh filled the Hummer. The fashion magazine was lowered to reveal the glossy, curled lip and narrowed blue eyes of Daphne Lear herself! She gave Carmen and Juni a sullen, appraising stare. Then she arched one perfect eyebrow and said, "Hello, Learjets!"

Carmen gasped at the insult. But before she could explain to Daphne that they were not hangers-on but hardworking bodyguards, the pop star had ducked behind her magazine once again. Daphne had nothing more to say to her bodyguards.

The Spy Kids–turned–Learjets finished the ride to the stadium in stunned silence.

A few hours later, Carmen and Juni found themselves shunted to the sidelines again. They were ordered to hover in the wings of the giant concert stage while Daphne performed her concert. They watched in awe as she belted out hit after hit, danced around the stage for hours without a break, and whizzed through no fewer than fourteen costume changes. The only constant in Daphne's mutating look was her necklace. The red gem went with every outfit, resting perfectly on her tanned throat.

And the audience couldn't get enough. They screamed out their adoration at the end of every song.

The only ones who didn't seem wowed were Daphne's entourage, who milled around back-stage, yammering into their cell phones about Daphne's late-night talk-show appearances and concert T-shirt designs.

"She's not a girl," Juni breathed into his sister's ear. "She's an *empire*."

"But isn't it funny that not one person here cares to listen to her actually *sing*?" Carmen mar-veled. She herself couldn't take her eyes off the charismatic pop sensation. Having just finished a wild dance number with a dozen backup dancers and soap bubbles that spewed all over the audi-ence, Daph was plunking herself onto a glittering carousel horse.

"All right, rockers," she announced. "Grab your sweeties, and get ready to slow-dance."

Then Daphne placed a hand over her heart and began to croon, *"I'm stuck on you-ooo-ooo-ooo!"*

The Spy Kids were transfixed—until, that is, Juni suddenly realized something.

"Y'know what's weird?" he whispered to his sister.

"*Shhh*, I'm listening," Carmen said, blinking a bit of moisture away from her eyes.

Juni, of course, didn't *shhh* at all.

"A lot of rock stars sound really bad in concert," Juni observed.

"Duh," Carmen said. "They only sound good on their albums—*after* some producers have made their voices sound perfect."

"Yeah, but Daphne Lear can actually *sing*," Juni said. "Her voice is really pretty."

"I guess that's what separates a flavor of the month from the next star," Carmen said with a shrug. Then she tried to return her attention to the show.

That was easier said than done. The cell phone–toting Learjets had bustled away, but now a bunch of FODs (Friends of Daphne) were beginning to crowd around the Spy Kids.

"*Oooh*, Daph looks *sooooo* cute," one of them cooed, pointing over Juni's shoulder toward the stage.

"I hope she remembered to invite Brandon Crushman to the show," another sighed. "He's *the* cutest guy in Outta Touch, which is *the* best boy band in the world. Daphne promised to introduce me to him!"

"Um, excuse me," Carmen grunted as one of

the teenagers elbowed her way in front of her. "But we're bodyguarding Miss Lear. Would you mind staying out of our line of vision?"

"Whatever," the offending girl snapped. She tugged at her sparkly minidress as she stepped aside. Then she looked Carmen up and down. Carmen smoothed her own outfit—cargo pants and a yellow OSS T-shirt—self-consciously.

"Nice ensemble," the girl sneered. "So very . . . sporty."

"So very annoying," Carmen muttered to her brother.

"So very hungry!" Juni responded.

"Huh?" Carmen said, eyeing the teenagers. "Now that you mention it, those girls *are* superskinny."

"Not them, *me*!" Juni complained. Then *he* pointed to the stage, or rather, to the wings on the opposite side of the stage. Beyond the curtains was a long table laden with brownies, sandwiches, smoothies, and other delectables for musicians and crew members to nibble on and drink. "*All* those snacks. It's driving me crazy."

Carmen rolled her eyes. Could Juni *ever* get his head out of the cookie jar? But before she could dis him in her usual way, she stopped herself. She smelled another deal!

"Tell you what," she said. "Let's guard Daphne in shifts. You let me escape this snotty scene, and I'll wait for Daph in her dressing room. After you escort her back there, you're off the hook. You can go snack to your heart's content."

"You got it!" Juni declared, shaking Carmen's hand emphatically.

A few minutes later, Carmen had reached Daphne's dressing room. Hesitantly, she poked her head through the door.

"Hello?" she called.

She was greeted with nothing but the lingering scents of Daphne's hair spray and perfume. Carmen recognized the fruity notes of Daffy, Daphne's signature cologne. She'd just recently sniffed a sample of it in a teen magazine.

And now I'm in Daphne Lear's *dressing room,* Carmen thought exultantly. Wow!

The Spy Girl skipped into the empty dressing room. She gawked at the photos lining the make-up mirror—snapshots of Daphne with a host of hot celebrities. She gaped at Daphne's bulging makeup kit. Reverentially, Carmen approached the megastar's groaning wardrobe rack. It was an explosion of hot-pink "pleather" and mint-colored marabou. The flash of sequins and rhinestones was intoxicating. Carmen couldn't resist reaching out to touch the shimmery velvets, satins, and silks.

Her eyes fell upon a coppery blouse hanging next to some classic, leopard-print leggings. Carmen's mouth dropped open.

That, she thought enviously, is the *coolest . . . out-fit . . . ever*!

She just *had* to try it on.

Carmen glanced at her spy watch. It was a new model of her most essential gizmo. In addition to being a satellite communications system, a weapon coordinator, a mapping device, and a dozen other gadgets, it *even* told time, as well as performing many other useful tasks.

And the watch showed Carmen that Daphne's show wouldn't be ending for another twenty minutes! So, with a gleeful giggle, Carmen ditched her OSS uniform and slipped on the slinky ensemble.

She also grabbed a long, blond wig from a shelf behind the wardrobe and planted it over her dark hair. Then she stood before Daphne's full-length mirror and gasped.

She *was* Daphne Lear. She was cool. And famous! And she could sing like nobody's business! Everybody wanted a piece of her!

Particularly, the somebody who'd slipped silently into the dressing room while Carmen's back was turned. The masked intruder was so silent and stealthy that Carmen didn't notice a thing—until the invader lunged for her neck!

CHAPTER 4

In the split second before the attacker's hands closed around Carmen's neck, her finely honed spy skills kicked in! She dodged to the left with such force she went flying! But she recovered quickly, landing with a neat somersault and springing to her feet, her fists raised.

Meanwhile, the intruder crashed to the dressing-room floor. The attacker—a masked woman clad entirely in black—stared at Carmen. Then she reared back on her hands and did a reverse hand-spring to get to *her* feet.

Uh-oh, Carmen thought. She's a professional. Time to evade. Carmen reached for her belt. With nimble fingers, she did a quick inventory of the half-dozen gadgets hanging from it.

Aha! Carmen thought as her hand landed on an innocuous-looking drinking straw. Perfect.

Carmen glanced around the dressing room. She saw a blank sheet of lavender stationery on the makeup table behind her. Grabbing the paper, Carmen stuffed it into her mouth and started chewing.

Blecch! she thought with a grimace. Daphne must have sprayed the paper with Daffy perfume!

But a good spy is never deterred by grossness. So Carmen kept chewing. When the paper was good and spit-soaked, she held the straw up to her mouth, tilted her head back, and spat!

And that was when something incredible happened. Because Carmen's drinking straw, of course, was not the sort one just picks up at a fast-food joint. It was an Uncle Machete Super Spitball Spitter— lined with a combination of Expansion Compound and superglue. By the time Carmen's spitball had traveled through the straw and hit the ceiling, it was the size of a bowling ball and as sticky as cement.

With that anchor in place, Carmen took her trusty Claw 'n' Cable from her belt. She aimed the claw at the spitball and threw it with all her strength. After the claw hit the paper wad with a sick *squelch*, Carmen hit the gizmo's retract button.

Zzzzziiiipp!

In less than a second, the cable was sucked back into the claw. And Carmen went up with it! She hovered beneath the high ceiling and glared down at the intruder.

She'll never reach me up here, Carmen thought with a satisfied cackle.

She watched the masked woman's eyes narrow as she gazed up at her.

Perhaps she's calculating how high she can jump, Carmen thought with satisfaction, and realizing she'll *never* reach me.

Or maybe she's trying to figure out how she'll get out of here without being placed under arrest.

Carmen was wrong on both counts.

Apparently, all the attacker wanted to do was check out Carmen's wardrobe! The woman's eyes skimmed carefully over the Spy Girl's cat-print pants and her shimmery blouse and finally came to rest at her neck.

Carmen frowned in confusion and quickly placed her hand on her neck. All she found there were her open shirt collar and a few strands of her blond wig.

Seeing the same thing, the invader let loose a disgusted harrumph. Then she began ignoring Carmen completely. Instead, she started prowling around the dressing room. She spotted a small, silver box on Daphne's makeup table. She scooped up the box and began to run for the dressing-room door!

Swiftly disengaging her Claw 'n' Cable, Carmen dropped to the floor with a thud.

"Halt, by order of the OSS!" she barked.

The intruder, of course, ignored her.

Time for another spitball, Carmen thought with a weary sigh. Swiping *another* perfume-soaked piece of stationery from Daphne's vanity, she chewed up the stinky ammo and raised her straw.

Ptoooooey!

Carmen spat the paper wad right at the silver box clutched in the attacker's hand.

Splatttttt!

It was a direct hit! When the spitball hit the wall, it took the woman's booty with it. The box was now wedged into its gummy surface!

The attacker gaped at her hand. An instant earlier, she'd been clutching a silver treasure box. Now, she held merely a fistful of spit-soaked paper.

"Ewww!" she squealed—before fleeing the dressing room altogether.

"Evil thwarted!" Carmen crowed, jumping around in excitement. "And on my first day on the job. Cool!"

"Cool?" said a throaty voice from the dressing room door. "I *so* don't think so."

Carmen stopped crowing.

And she stopped jumping.

Then she turned toward the voice with a gulp.

Daphne was standing in the doorway. A fluffy towel was slung around her neck and she was holding her super-high-heeled shoes in one hand. She was staring at the giant spitballs on the ceiling and wall.

"What are those disgusting things?" she demanded.

Juni and a few other members of Daphne's entourage crowded into the dressing room behind the pop star. Juni gazed up at the spitballs and grinned. Carmen could almost read his mind: Gross! As in, cool!

"Um, well, it's kind of funny, actually," Carmen stuttered. "They're, uh, giant spitballs."

"Funny?" Daphne asked with an arched eyebrow. "You think trashing my dressing room is funny?"

Carmen gulped again. One of the most famous people in the world was totally annoyed with her! For most twelve-year-old girls, this would have been the perfect time for a major meltdown.

But Carmen Cortez was made of tougher stuff than that. In fact, with that last gulp, she seemed to swallow her nervousness. And when it disappeared, rage stepped in to take its place! Suddenly, Carmen didn't care how famous and glamorous Daphne

Lear was. She'd just saved her silver box from being swiped! And from the looks of the box's heavy-duty lock, there was clearly something highly valuable hidden inside it!

"Actually, I think it's a hoot!" Carmen declared. "But then again, I'm trained to laugh at evil. You, however, might be alarmed to hear what happened during your concert."

With that, Carmen told Daphne the entire story, from the attacker's first lunge for her neck to the attempt to steal the box. When Daphne seemed unimpressed, Carmen marched over to the spitball on the wall and wrenched the silver box from it. With an expression of triumph—and a little defiance—Carmen handed the box to Daphne.

Daphne pulled a tiny, golden key out of her vanity drawer and unbolted the box's tiny padlock. Then she popped the silver cube open.

Eagerly, Carmen peered inside.

It was empty!

"Uh-huh," Daphne confirmed with a curled lip. "So basically, you *spat* on my dressing room in order to rescue a worthless jewelry box. I guess the OSS doesn't train 'em like they used to!"

"Hee, hee, hee." Daphne's high school buddies tittered behind their hands.

"People!" exclaimed an impatient voice from the hallway. A moment later, Nigel Knot pushed his way into the dressing room.

"Daphne!" he gasped. "Why haven't you changed yet? You've got an autograph-signing in seven minutes, followed by six late-night radio spots. Hup, hup!"

"Sorry, Nigel," Daphne said, giving Carmen a steely stare. "A little 'guard' got in my way. But she was just on her way out. Weren't you, Carmen? Oh, and, if you're not too busy, you know, *guarding* me and all, would you mind getting my outfit dry-cleaned? Next time you want to play dress up, you might ask me first!"

Carmen felt her cheeks flush bright pink. She glanced around the dressing room. A dozen pairs of eyes were trained directly upon her. And the looks were *not* kind.

"Whatever!" Carmen cried, before storming out of Daphne's dressing room.

"Carmen!" Juni called out. He pounded after her.

But Carmen didn't like anybody to see her upset—especially her brother. So she broke into a sprint and darted down one of the stadium's circuitous corridors.

CHAPTER 5

Carmen found a hiding place far beneath the concert stage. She sank to a seat on an oversized snare drum and let loose a small snuffle . . . followed by a giant sob. Before she knew it, she was totally in tears.

Stop it, she scolded herself. Spies don't cry! Crying is completely uncool!

Suddenly, a quiet voice behind her made Carmen jump.

"I know what you're thinking."

Carmen gasped and wiped the wetness from her cheeks. Then she turned around.

"Oh, Juni," she sighed.

Her brother was standing before her, looking troubled. In one hand, he held a box of tissues. In the other, he had a giant chocolate-chip muffin that he'd swiped from the snack table.

"You're thinking that spies don't cry," Juni continued. "But look at Dad. He's Mr. Waterworks.

You know what Mom always says: 'Spaniards . . .'"

"'. . . Are *very* emotional,'" Carmen finished, with a small giggle. She swiped a tissue from Juni's box and took the gooey muffin. As a way of thanking him for cheering her up—without getting all gushy—Carmen split the sweet in two and gave half to Juni. Her snackaholic bro promptly took a big, chocolaty bite.

"Don't listen to what that Daphne says," Juni said as Carmen blew her nose and blinked the redness out of her eyes. "The girl's got pop star–itis. She thinks the world revolves around her."

"In a way, a world *does* revolve around her," Carmen pointed out. "A world of interviews and merchandise and an entourage that never leaves her alone!"

"Tell me about it," Juni said. "That Nigel Knot is glued to her like fish on chips."

"If she wasn't so mean, I'd almost feel sorry for her," Carmen said.

"Nah, I'm feeling more sorry for us," Juni said, his mouth full of muffin. "Our valuable spy skills are being wasted! Like you said, Daphne's Learjets never leave her side. What does she need OSS bodyguards for anyway?"

ZZZZzzzzztttttt-sputterrrr.

No sooner had the words left Juni's mouth than all the lights went out! The corridor went pitch-black!

"What happened?" Juni asked, a small tremor in his voice.

"Probably a power surge," Carmen said, getting to her feet and searching her utility belt for a glow stick. "After all, Daphne's concert calls for major pyrotechnics. Did you see that giant Lite Brite simulation? It alone probably used a million watts!"

Carmen found her glow stick and gave it a snap. A burst of eerie, green light filled the corridor.

"Finish your muffin and let's find our way back to the dressing room," Carmen said with a sigh. "Duty calls."

Aaiiiiigggh-eeeeeeeee!

The sudden scream was raspy and guttural. And it echoed through every corner of the arena.

"Duty calls—literally!" Juni cried. "Sounds like someone's in trouble!"

He began to dash down the hallway. Carmen followed close behind, holding up the glow stick to light their way.

"At least it's not Daphne," Carmen breathed, as she chased behind Juni. "No way did that raspy voice belong to our snippy songbird."

"Who cares who it is?" Juni called out. "It's rescue time!"

"Tscha!" Carmen cried.

In fact, the idea of doing something *right* on this mission completely cheered her up! By the time the Spy Kids arrived backstage, Carmen was ready to rumble—until she saw something that chilled her to the bone! A bunch of stricken Learjets were huddled around Daphne's dressing-room door. They looked pale and confused and totally freaked out.

Okay, let's put that "I'm all cheered up" idea on hold, Carmen thought, with dread. It looks like something *has* happened to Daphne!

While Carmen stopped in her tracks and went white, Juni sprang into crisis mode.

"OSS! Clear the way," he barked to the entourage. "We need to get through to Miss Lear."

He grabbed Carmen by the elbow and dragged her through the crowd. When the Spy Kids finally made their way into the dressing room, they saw Daphne sitting at her vanity.

Tears were streaming down her cheeks.

Her hair was a total mess.

Several of her makeup bottles had capsized, spilling pink, glittery stuff all over the floor.

It didn't look good!

"I know first aid," Juni cried. Yanking a stetho-scope from his cargo pants pocket, he slung the instrument around his neck and dashed over to the pop star. Briskly, he began ordering her to wiggle her fingers and toes. Then he grabbed her wrist and took her pulse.

"Mmm-hmmm, fascinating," Juni announced. He whipped a tongue depressor out of his utility belt. "Now, how many tongue depressors am I hold-ing up?"

"One!" Daphne sputtered.

"Excellent," Juni said. "Say, 'Ahhhh!'"

"Aaaaaahhh!" Daphne screamed. "What are you doing? There's nothing wrong with me!"

"Why didn't you just say so?" Juni complained. "So, what happened?"

"I was robbed, that's what happened," Daphne rasped, clutching her throat. Her . . . *bare* throat. "My necklace. It's *goooooone!*"

"Whoa!" whispered one of the FODs. "Daph never goes anywhere without wearing her ruby necklace."

Carmen stepped forward. She was still pale and trembling—she'd totally failed this assignment! But she wanted to make amends.

"Daphne," she announced. "This is my fault. I was supposed to be guarding you. So I want you to know, I will pay to have your necklace replaced from my own allowance."

Daphne merely shook her head. "You don't understand," Daphne cried. Her sobs had made her voice as scratchy as sandpaper. "That necklace can't be replaced. And furthermore, the show can't go on. Nigel!"

"Yes, Daph!" Nigel piped up. He was perched, of course, right at his star's elbow.

"Cancel my next tour date," Daphne ordered him. "I can't perform!"

With a fresh burst of sobs, Daphne popped out of her chair and ran to the bathroom, locking herself inside.

When, after several minutes, Daphne didn't emerge, the stunned Learjets began to drift away from the dressing room. Soon, the only ones who remained were the Spy Kids, Nigel, and Daphne's mother.

"Cancel her next concert?" Nigel squeaked to Ginny Jo. "*Cancel*? But that just isn't done! We'll be ruined!"

"I'll try to talk her into going back on the road," Ginny Jo said. "But you know my little girl. When she gets a notion in her head—even a crazy, selfish one—there's no talkin' her out of it!"

"Talk about unsupportive," Carmen whispered to Juni. The Spy Kids left the dressing room. With their heads hanging, they drifted down a backstage corridor—until a sound made them stop in their tracks. A horrible sound!

"Had a dream about you, scraping bubble gum off the bottom of your shoe. Just like that goo—I'm stuck on you-ooo-ooo-ooo!"

"Ouch!" Juni said. "Did you hear that?"

"It sounds like a lemur with laryngitis!" Carmen said with a nod.

"Or a cat with a cold," Juni said.

"But how many lemurs or cats know the lyrics to Daphne's biggest hit, 'Ooey, Gooey Me'?" Carmen asked.

She looked up at the source of the sound. It was a ceiling grate leading to an air-conditioning duct.

"What's on the other side of this wall, Juni?" Carmen asked slowly.

Juni peeked around the corridor's corner.

"I think it's Daphne's bathroom!" he said.

Whooooosssh!

"And that's the sound of her shower," Carmen exclaimed.

Juni got a scheming look in his eye.

"This is definitely a case for the Eve's-Dropper!" he declared.

"Well, you would know, wouldn't you?" Carmen said drily. "Okay, break the scheming little snake out."

Juni pulled the Eve's-Dropper out of his pocket. Then he popped his adaptable joystick out of his spy watch.

Once Juni had programmed the Eve's-Dropper to transmit its recording to his watch, he sent the snake slithering into the grate. In seconds, the kids could hear the singing loud and clear.

Of course, "singing" was a generous term for such raspy rock and roll.

"I'm stuck on you-ooo-ooo-ooo! . . ." the voice shrilled.

"That can't be Daphne," Carmen said. "She sounds awful!"

"Who else could it be?" Juni said. "Daphne's voice is shot! And she's got some major explaining to do!"

CHAPTER 6

When Daphne emerged from her steam-filled bathroom a half hour later, there were guests waiting for her in her dressing room.

But these were no fans.

Or Learjets.

These were no-nonsense spies! And they were on a mission to find the truth!

"What's the word, hummingbird?" Carmen asked the pop star snidely.

"Ex-*cuse* me?" Daphne said. She flopped down at her makeup table and began toweling her wet hair. She glared at the Spy Kids and said, "I'm no bird."

"Oh, that's right," Carmen corrected herself. "How could you be? After all, birds can sing!"

Daphne's towel froze in mid-rub. She peeked out from beneath the fluffy terry cloth at the Spy Kids.

"What are you talking about?" she asked darkly.

"Simply this," Juni said, holding up his spy watch.

With the press of a button, the Eve's-Dropper's recording of Daphne singing—make that squawking—filled the dressing room. After a few seconds, Juni turned the watch off. Then he gave the pop star a hard, accusing stare.

Daphne's sparkly blue eyes widened and her honey-colored skin went pale—for an instant. Then she shook her panic away and scowled.

"I don't know who that is, or why you think I care," she pouted. "Haven't you *kids* done enough damage for one night? First you allow my necklace to be snatched off my very own neck. Now you have to harass me, too?"

"There's no harassment in the truth," Carmen spat. "And the truth is, Daphne, this is you."

She reached out and pressed the play button on Juni's spy watch. Once again, the room was filled with a screeching soprano stumbling through "Ooey, Gooey Me."

As the squawks echoed painfully in their ears, the spies and the star stared at each other defiantly. They were locked in a standoff! But finally, Daphne caved.

"Turn it off! Turn it off!" she screamed, clapping her hands over her ears. "It's awful!"

Gratefully, Juni complied. That horrible music

had been making him a bit queasy! (Or maybe it was all the snacks he'd devoured.)

Meanwhile, Daphne slumped onto her dressing-room couch and gazed at the floor. Tears welled up in her eyes. She refused to look up, until Carmen sat down next to her and put a sympathetic hand on her shoulder.

"That *was* you, wasn't it?" Carmen said softly.

Slowly, Daphne nodded.

"Can you explain to us what's going on?" Carmen asked gently. "Maybe we can help."

Again, Daphne nodded. But before she began to speak, she reached into a bag sitting on the floor next to the couch. From it, she pulled a small embroidery hoop. A piece of fabric embroidered with the motto "Home, Sweet Home" was stretched inside the hoop. Daph also pulled out a brown paper sack. She held it out to the Spy Kids.

"Horehound candy?" she offered.

Queasiness forgotten, Juni dug a handful of the hard candies from the bag. Daphne popped one into her own mouth, then plucked a needle from a pincushion in her bag. She began to work on the embroidery.

"Cross-stitching always helps me think," she explained to the surprised kids. "I don't have time to do it too often, being so busy and all. Plus, Nigel says it's too country—cross-stitching and eating horehound candy. He doesn't want any paparazzi to get a picture of me being non-edgy. But what can I say? You can take the girl out of Alabama, but you can't take Alabama out of the girl."

Again, Carmen was filled with an ache of sympathy.

It must be awful, she thought, never being allowed just to be yourself!

"Are you ready to tell us about your voice?" she asked.

Daphne nodded. Then she pointed at her bare neck.

"My necklace," she said with a heavy sigh, "wasn't just any old necklace."

"What was it?" Juni wondered.

"It was the C-3," Daphne announced gravely.

"Huh?"

"That's short for Charlatan Chanteuse Crystal," Daphne continued. She kept her eyes down and stitched feverishly as she spoke. "It's more secret than the OSS."

"What does it do?" Juni said.

"It makes you sing like an angel," Daphne admitted. "With that magical stone around your neck, anyone would sound like, well, like I did on stage tonight. The C-3 was created by an ancient mystic—forged from the eyeballs of songbirds."

"Ewww!" Juni blurted. "Eyeballs?"

"Shhh," Carmen said. She knew that confessing that secret was hard for Daphne. She didn't want her to clam up because of Juni's outburst. "Go ahead," Carmen said to Daphne.

"The C-3 has been in circulation for generations," Daphne continued. "It's been passed down from opera divas to Broadway belters to rock stars. Whoever held the jewel was guaranteed instant stardom."

"Whoa," Carmen breathed. "Who gave it to you?"

"Oh, I can't tell you," Daphne said. "That's top secret. All I can say is, she was a very kind woman who understood what it feels like to be a simple, Southern girl who wants nothing more than to sing. She thought I had enough character to handle all the fame and adoration the C-3 would bring me."

At that, Daphne hung her head down further.

"I guess I let her down," Daphne said with a quiet sob. "I've been a totally obnoxious diva. I treated *you* horribly, for instance."

"You kinda did," Juni agreed. He looked at his

sister. He could see that she was thinking the same thing he was—it'd be completely satisfying to rub salt into the pop star's wounds right now. But Juni was still working on that making-the-parents-proud thing. So he added, "But we forgive you, Daphne."

"Bygones," Carmen agreed.

Daphne flashed the Spy Kids a grateful smile.

"You were under the C-3's spell," Juni noted, with a shrug. "You didn't really know what you were doing."

"But I *am* responsible for being cocky," Daphne said, her grin evaporating quickly. "*And* I was totally careless with the C-3. In centuries, this is the first time it's ever been stolen. It's a tragedy!"

"Yes, someone else will be hitting the top of the charts soon," Carmen said. "But Daphne, I've got to be honest with you. It seems like being a normal teenager again might not be so bad for you. You could go back to school, have friends who aren't just angling for an introduction to Brandon Crushman, go home to Alabama. It does seem like you miss it."

Carmen nodded at Daphne's "Home, Sweet Home" cross-stitch.

"You don't understand," Daphne .cried. "This isn't just about me and my ruined career. This is about the power of the C-3. Until now, it's only been used to attain musical stardom. But in the wrong hands, it could easily be used . . . for evil!"

"What do you mean?" Juni asked breathlessly.

"It's hard to explain," Daphne said. "After all, nobody but that ancient mystic knows exactly how the Charlatan Chanteuse Crystal works. But it does seem to do more than make your voice beautiful. It injects your songs with charm. It fills people's hearts with adoration. It makes them want to do . . . whatever you say. Until now, the keepers of the C-3 have only said harmless things like, 'Listen to this album I made,' or 'Come to my concert.' But somebody else could use it to—"

"Make people commit crimes," Juni said darkly.

"Or take over the world," Carmen cried. She jumped to her feet. "This is big! We have to find out who stole that jewel and get it back before they do some serious damage!"

"You're right," Daphne said with a shuddery sigh. "That's all that matters right now."

Carmen bit her lip and gazed at Daphne.

"Well . . . that's not *all* that matters," she said. "Daph, the C-3 was definitely not the most honest way to become a rock star. But if we'd been better bodyguards, it wouldn't have been stolen. What's more, I can see your heart's in the right place. You just wanted to sing. To make people happy."

"Yeah! That's all I've ever wanted," Daphne cried, letting her cross-stitch fall back into her bag. "But I made a complete mess of things."

"Well, maybe not a complete mess," Carmen said. "What if we made a deal with you?"

"A deal?" Daphne and Juni asked in unison.

"If we can find the C-3, we'll return it to you," Carmen proposed. "You just have to promise to start taking voice lessons—to become a star through hard work and not some magic gem. Eventually, you won't need the C-3 to carry your career. And when that happens, you'll need to destroy the crystal. That way, it'll never fall into the wrong hands again."

"Sounds like a plan!" Daphne cried happily. She sprang to her feet and shook Carmen's hand. But then she looked troubled again.

"The only prob is, how will I keep my career afloat while you guys hunt down the crystal?" she wondered. "With every canceled concert, my cred is going to crumble!"

"Get laryngitis," Juni proposed. "Or appendicitis! Or, hey, how 'bout tendinitis?!"

Carmen rolled her eyes. Then she turned to Daphne.

"You get the point," she said. "Stall 'em! And meanwhile, we don't have another minute to lose in our C-3 search."

"In fact," she continued, eyeing Juni craftily, "I think it's time we call in the troops!"

CHAPTER 7

Mere minutes after Carmen and Juni issued their red alert, complete with a briefing on the C-3, "the troops" answered the call. They pulled up outside the concert arena in a deep-purple jeep with tinted windows.

As the Spy Kids made their way toward the car, the passenger-side window opened smoothly. A woman with ginger-colored curls and a crinkly-eyed grin poked her head through the opening. It was their mother.

"Hi, sweeties!" she called out. "Hop on in! I have snacks for you!"

Oh, man, Carmen thought, glancing around quickly. I hope nobody heard that. They'll think we're "mama's spies."

The Spy Kids hurried over to the jeep.

"Mom," Carmen said as she tumbled into the vehicle's backseat. "We're on a top secret mission to save the world. We don't have time for snacks and bedtime stories and stuff like that."

"Hey, speak for yourself," Juni protested. His face lit up as Mom passed him a small bag of home-made cookies. "Thanks, Mom."

"Actually, your father made them," Mom replied with a wink.

From the driver's seat, Dad shrugged sheep-ishly. "Hey, I'm just trying to be a cool dad," he said. "Speaking of . . . check this out!"

Dad reached out and flipped a switch on the dashboard. Suddenly, purple neon lights lining the windshield began flashing wildly. Music began pounding out of the stereo. The bass beat thumped so hard the Spy Kids could feel it in their stomachs!

What's more, the jeep began bouncing around like a rubber ball!

"Oh, the humiliation," Carmen cried, strug-gling to be heard over the superloud tunes. "This souped-up car is *so* 1996!"

"What?" Dad protested. "I thought these wheels would fit into your new rock-and-roll lifestyle. They're, how do you say . . . *phat*!"

"Parents," Juni muttered, shaking his head. "So clueless."

Carmen tried to be more diplomatic.

"The car's really cool, Dad," she said carefully. "But wouldn't it be easier for you and Mom to, um, work if we cut down on the reverb, just a bit?"

"Oh, no," Dad protested loudly. "Your mother and I, we're down with the youth. We can chill just fine."

Juni gaped at his father. Then he hissed to Carmen, "They've completely lost it!"

Carmen nodded in agreement—and horror.

"Okay, well, if you're not too busy *chillin'*, Mom and Dad," she sighed, "we really need to focus on tracking down the C-3."

"Right on!" Dad said. He hit the gas and the throbbing jeep began rolling and bouncing down the street. "What do you think we're doing?"

"Hotdogging?" Juni answered. "Cruising?"

"If this were just an ordinary loud jeep, yes," Dad said. "But this car was customized by your Uncle Machete!"

"You mean . . ." Carmen said.

"It's a spy gadget in disguise!" Dad finished Carmen's thought. "It's called the Charm Pop. With every bounce, this baby is sending out powerful, sweeping, radar waves. And those waves are adjusted to 1,300 gigawatts."

"With just a dash of nuclear peptide action," Mom added with a sly grin.

"But that's the secret, government formula for searching out cosmic activity!" Carmen said realizing the danger.

"Right you are, Carmenita," Dad said. "Our magic-detecting radar can scan over a three-hundred-mile radius! I bet we'll be picking up a signal from the C-3 any second now."

"That's brilliant!" Carmen sputtered.

Byrrrr! Byrrr! Byrrr!

A sirenlike alarm was blaring from the dashboard. The Cortezes peered at the jeep's computer. As the alarm died down, a hazy, black-and-white image began to appear on its screen. Data popped onto the computer screen, next to the cloudy picture.

"Oh, rats," Mom said, as the picture—a giant, colorful arc with a black cauldron at one end—faded away. "That wasn't the C-3. It was just a rainbow with a pot of gold at the end."

"What?" Carmen and Juni shrieked. "Are you serious?"

"Children, you know Uncle Machete's gizmos," Dad said apologetically. "Full of glitches. The Charm Pop is going to pick up on *all* cosmic activity. Not just that of the C-3."

Byrrrr! Byrrr! Byrrr!

"There's another one!" Juni cried excitedly. "What is it?"

"Hmmm," Mom said, once again deciphering the data on the screen. "Nope, this isn't the C-3, either. It's just a tall, hairy guy with really big feet."

"I wonder what *that's* about?" Carmen said.

The spies' jeep bounced onward.

The alarm blared again.

And again! It picked up a bright, green meteor and a giant stack of stones that seemed to defy gravity.

But no C-3.

After several more minutes of fruitless searching, Juni sighed in frustration.

"The thrill of the hunt has lost its thrill," he said, flopping back in his seat. "I need a little cartoon break."

Pulling a remote control from his armrest, Juni pointed it at the tiny, satellite television that hung from the jeep's ceiling. With a yawn, he started channel surfing.

Juni was just about to flip past a soap opera when suddenly, the show disappeared all by itself! It was replaced by a cheery TV-news reporter, clutching a microphone. A banner on the screen read: SPECIAL REPORT—BREAKING NEWS!

The reporter was standing in a large room bustling with clapping, cheering people. And looking down upon those people from a small stage was a very tall, very big-boned woman with a cottony, ash-blond, bouffant hairdo. Her red lipstick was painted on with razor-sharp precision and her eyebrows were plucked into severe, black arches. Even on TV, you could see the intensity of her steely, blue eyes and the stiffness of her broad smile. Modestly, she tried to wave away her fans' cheers. But that only made them hoot louder.

"What's going on there?" Mom wondered, peering back over the top of the front seat to catch a glimpse of the TV.

The newscaster provided an instant answer.

"Hello, I'm Kitty Cork," she said with a sweet smile. "And I'm reporting to you, *live*, from Washington, D.C. Tell me, folks. When I say the name Middie Prole, what do you think of?"

The reporter paused dramatically. Then she chirped, "Nothing, right? Yes, very few people have ever heard of the statuesque Texan standing behind me. Until yesterday, she was working as a cabinet member for the mayor of Turtlekill, Texas, population 2,300. Back in eighth grade, Ms. Prole was apparently vice president of the student council. Other than that, this C-list politician is virtually unknown!

"But believe me," the reporter burbled on. "You'll be hearing a lot about Middie Prole in the days and weeks to come. She has just announced that she is running for president! What's more, she's got a platform that people are calling—and I quote—'bewitchingly brilliant.'"

"'Bewitchingly brilliant'?" Carmen repeated. "That's an interesting choice of words."

"And here's the real kick in the pants, folks," the reporter said in closing. "Only a couple of hours into her campaign, the oh-so-obscure Middie Prole's initial approval ratings are sky-high. In fact, our on-staff historian, Morris Burns-Goodfellow, assures us that Middie Prole's instant stardom has made political history. I'm Kitty Cork, reporting to you live for MYPQ. Now, back to our regularly scheduled programming."

"Huh," Juni said with a shrug. "If I were old enough to vote, that news report might have been really interesting."

Then he aimed his remote control, ready to resume his cartoon hunt.

"Wait!" Carmen said suddenly, snatching the remote-control device from Juni's hand. "I want to see something."

"Hey, I had the remote," Juni complained. "You just want to find some mushy, made-for-TV movie."

"Puh-leeze," Carmen said, rolling her eyes. "If you recall, boob-tube brain, we are spying here. And I have a hunch about this 'bewitching' politician."

Carmen pressed the TiVo button on the remote. (Hey, spies don't always need *spy* gadgets.) She rewound the news report they'd just watched. When the camera zoomed in on Middie Prole, Carmen hit PAUSE.

Then she zoomed in closer.

And closer.

"Whoa, speaking of being so 1996," Mom said as Middie Prole's angular face filled the TV screen. "Those painted-on eyebrows are scarily retro!"

"I'm more interested in her antique jewelry," Carmen said breathlessly.

She pointed at Middie Prole's high-collared white blouse. Between the top two buttons, there was a slight bulge.

When Carmen zoomed in even closer, the spies could just barely discern a flash of color beneath the white fabric.

That color was red.

The sudden star was clearly wearing a large, red gem beneath her blouse.

"Folks," Carmen announced. "I think we have ourselves a winner."

CHAPTER 8

The moment Carmen pinpointed Middie Prole as the C-3 thief, Dad flipped off the Charm Pop's booming, thumping cosmic radar.

"Great spying!" he declared. "What's more, Middie Prole will be easy to track down. All we have to do is turn on the news!"

"And when we find her, we'll pose as campaign volunteers," Carmen proposed.

"Another excellent idea," Mom said. "Okay, what do we know about political operatives?"

"They feed entirely on cheap coffee and glazed doughnuts," Juni piped up. "That's a known fact. Yum!"

"They also keep insane hours," Carmen said. "They never sleep!"

"And wardrobe?" Dad scoffed. "Wrinkled khakis and blue shirts. Cheap ties. Conservative haircuts."

Mom gave her family an appraising look. In her own body-skimming spy vest and knee-high boots, she looked pretty slick. Dad's dark shades and slicked-back hair were also too cool for school. And the Spy Kids? Forget about it. In their cargo pants, high-tech OSS shirts and electronic gear, they would never be mistaken for ordinary kids, much less junior policy wonks.

"We're *definitely*," Mom pointed out, "going to need some disguises."

Minutes later, the Cortezes pulled into the gear garage at OSS headquarters. Dad swapped the bouncing Charm Pop for an ordinary minivan. Then the spies headed for Wardrobe.

While Mom chose outfits for her husband and herself, Juni went to the Iron-On Lab. The small room was dominated by a computer outfitted with the latest in image-enhancement programs. That computer was connected to a giant, robotic arm clutching a clothes iron.

Grabbing the computer mouse, Juni started drawing. Quickly, he rigged up a perfect picture of Middie Prole: scary, arching eyebrows; blood-red lips; and all. Beneath the image, he dashed off the slogan:

```
She'll help you meet your goals
   or get off the dole,
```

She'll even rid you of
unsightly moles;
But only if you vote for . . .
MIDDIE PROLE!

Juni tinted the entire affair in shades of red, white, and blue and laid a couple of kid-sized T-shirts on the ironing board. Then he hit PRINT.

Sssssssssssssss!

The robotic iron skimmed over the T-shirts, releasing a dramatic billow of steam and transferring Middie Prole's image and campaign slogan onto the fabric. In seconds, Juni was peeling his and Carmen's costumes off the ironing board. Then he went to meet his sister in Hair and Makeup.

When he arrived, Carmen had already teased her shiny, dark hair into a tangle that just screamed, "I spent last night sacked out on the campaign bus."

Now she was brushing gray powder beneath her eyes to simulate dark circles. Juni tossed her a T-shirt and got to work on his own look. He chose some black-rimmed glasses from the spectacles bank and parted his unruly, red curls in the middle.

As he completed his styling, Mom and Dad walked in. Mom was wearing a bubble-gum-pink suit and a matching headband. Dad was decked out in perfectly wrinkled khakis and a crooked, polyester tie.

"We're total political geeks," Juni said with a grin. "Ready for action."

With a determined grin of her own, Mom thrust out her hand. Carmen slapped her hand on top of Mom's. Then Juni and Dad added their hands to the stack as well.

"Who are we?" Dad asked.

"The Cortezes," his family shouted.

"And what do we do?"

"We save the world!" Mom, Carmen, and Juni cried.

"I'm sure the minivan's all gassed up and ready for us," Carmen said as the spies broke apart. "Let's go!"

"Yes, let's," a voice sang out.

Carmen spun around—and gasped. She felt as though she were looking in the mirror! She was staring at a teenager with dark, wavy hair just like her own. The girl also looked pale and tired. She wore sensible shoes, wrinkled clothes, and a campaign button that read GO, GO, GO! MIDDIE PROLE! Slung over her shoulder was a stuffed overnight bag.

Had Carmen's long-lost twin suddenly appeared

to surprise her? No. This was a certain pop star in disguise!

"Daphne?" Carmen sputtered. Over the camouflaged singer's shoulder, Carmen noticed the hunched, retreating figure of Daphne's tutor, Charlotte, who, incidentally, needed no disguise to look like a geek. "What are you doing here?"

"I'm here to help!" Daphne declared. "Since you're still on my bodyguard detail, I was able to get your mission info from the OSS. When they told me who had the C-3, I couldn't just sit back and let you do all the work. This is my fight, too!"

"And Charlotte's?" Juni asked, stepping forward to eye the tutor.

"Well, I'm only sixteen," Daphne said with a shrug. "I am not allowed to travel without a chaperone. Charlotte is so—um—easygoing, she made the most sense. I told her all about the C-3 on the drive over here."

"Uh-huh," Charlotte said quietly. "It was a very interesting story."

Carmen and Juni raised their eyebrows. That was the first time they'd ever heard the shy instructor speak.

"What did you tell the other people in your entourage?" Carmen asked Daphne.

"Mum's the word," Daphne assured the spies. "I told them—well, I whispered it, actually—that I had a terrible case of stress-induced laryngitis. I insisted that I needed a vacation to get my voice back. As far as they know, Charlotte and I are away vegging on the beach."

Mom stepped forward with a sympathetic frown.

"I hate to say this, honey," she said. "But maybe you *should* go veg on the beach. I appreciate your wanting to help, but this mission could be dangerous. It requires the skills of highly trained spies who've mastered karate, kung fu, and countless other fighting techniques; who speak dozens of languages; and who are masters of disguise and sneakiness."

"Spies like us," Juni said proudly.

Daphne nodded sadly.

"I guess you're right," she said, turning to leave the Hair and Makeup room. She paused and looked over her shoulder.

"Can I just say one thing before I go?" she asked.

"Of course," Dad said generously.

"Hi-yah!" Daphne screamed. She grabbed Juni by the shoulders, twisted him into a half nelson choke hold and flipped him over her head onto a pile of laundry.

She announced something—in Chinese—and dusted off her hands.

"Wha—what?" Juni said blearily as Mom helped him to his feet.

"She said, 'How do you like them apples?' in perfect Chinese," Carmen stated with wide eyes.

"That's my Cantonese dialect," Daphne said. "But I could also do Mandarin if you like."

"Where did you learn all that?" Juni sputtered, shaking off the last bit of wooziness.

"Hollywood!" Daphne said, with a grin. "Didn't you see my crossover movie hit, *The Grid*? Before we filmed the flick, the director brought in action choreographers from Hong Kong. All of us actors spent six months in training. It was fun! And along the way, I picked up a little Chinese."

"Well, then," Mom said, giving her family a flustered look. "I guess for you, going on a spy mission will seem like . . . a day at the beach!"

"Does that mean I get to go with you guys?" Daphne asked excitedly.

"That's what that means," Dad said, with a twinkle in his eye. "But, Daphne, if you're going to spy with us, you have to go by our rules. We will tolerate no divalike behavior on our mission; is that clear?"

"Understood," Daphne said with a sweet smile. She began to unzip her overnight bag. "I guess that means I should ditch all the gourmet goodies and expensive Italian sodas I brought for us to snack on, huh? After all, it is *diva* grub."

"Oh, I wouldn't act *too* hastily," Juni cried. He grabbed Daphne's bag before she could begin unpacking the snacks. "Why don't I inspect these in the van? You never know when gourmet snacks might come in handy on a mission!"

CHAPTER 9

By the next morning, the spies, Daphne, and Charlotte had infiltrated Middie Prole's campaign headquarters—a shabby Washington, D.C., storefront outfitted with little more than a couple of offices, a phone, a computer bank, and a bevy of coffee machines.

The spies were stationed all over the office. With Juni munching his way through a box of chocolate doughnuts, Dad swilling bad coffee, Carmen and Daphne stuffing envelopes, and Mom chirpily answering the phones, they blended in perfectly.

Now they just had to wait for Middie Prole to arrive.

They waited.

And waited.

And waited some more.

Carmen sighed as she reached for her third towering stack of Middie Prole leaflets. Her fingers were covered with paper cuts and her tongue was gummy from excessive envelope-licking.

"Wow," Carmen whispered to Daphne. "Being a campaign volunteer sure is tedious work. You gotta respect people who do this for real! Especially when they're not campaigning for an evil impostor."

"I know," Daphne said, licking an envelope of her own. Pensively, she looked at the disheveled workers bustling around the office. They were arranging Middie Prole's campaign appearances, fielding press interview requests, and phoning rich people to ask for donations.

"These people think they're saving the world by getting their candidate to the White House," Daphne said sagely. "But they should be careful. Because if there's anything I've learned from my rock-star years, it's that power is intoxicating. Power corrupts."

"And that's *without* the help of the Charlatan Chanteuse Crystal," Carmen said with a shudder. "Scary. I just hope we get the C-3 back from Middie Prole before she can do any real damage!"

No sooner had the words left Carmen's mouth than an excited rustling began to travel through the office. One woman hung up her phone abruptly and rushed to make a fresh pot of coffee. A young man straightened his tie and tucked several file folders beneath his arm. Everyone began gravitating toward the front door, chattering excitedly.

Shooting each other looks that said, "This is it!" the spies joined the throng at the glass door. Clearly, their candidate was about to arrive.

The crowd waited.

And waited.

And waited some more.

Finally, when the suspense became excruciating, a string of sleek cars pulled up to the curb outside. Several security agents leaped out of the first and last cars. Then, from the glittering black town car in the middle of the motorcade, the formidable form of Middie Prole emerged.

She strode in to the headquarters office to the cheers of her campaign workers. Smiling with all the genuineness of a plastic doll, Prole waved the adoration away.

"I'll give her this," Juni whispered to his sister. "The lady *knows* how to make an entrance. She's a master manipulator!"

As if to prove Juni's point, Middie Prole paused dramatically. And then . . . she spoke.

"I just want to thank y'all for working so hard," she brayed in a thick, Texan accent.

"You might think you're campaigning for Middie Prole," she continued. "But you're doing more than that. You're working for the American people—for every man, woman, and child in this great country! That . . . and jobs at the White House, once I'm elected."

"Yahoo!" the campaign workers cried.

"Now let's *all* get back to work," Prole cried, resting several of her long, red fingernails on her throat.

At least, her campaign workers *thought* she was resting her fingertips on her throat. But the spies knew that she was actually tapping the round lump beneath her turtleneck sweater—the C-3! Prole was wearing the proof that she was a thief and a deceiver and a power-grabber and lots of other really nasty things.

Now the spies just had to come up with a fool-proof way to get the gem back from her.

As each spy silently pondered various solutions, the young worker with the file folders sidled up to Middie Prole.

"Uh, Ms. Prole," he quavered. "I have this morning's press clippings about the campaign. Would you like to review them?"

"Indeed I would, son," Prole said loudly. She snatched the folders, crammed full of newspaper and magazine articles, from him.

"I'll look these over in my office," Prole said, marching solidly toward one of the cubicles. A throng of eager-beaver campaigners trailed after her, until Prole reached the doorway.

"Aw, now, ladies and gentlemen," she protested with her trademark stiff smile. "You *know* how I hate to be the center of attention. If you hover around me while I'm reading articles about myself, I'll be embarrassed! Could I trouble you for a few minutes of privacy?"

"Oh, yes, ma'am," the workers chorused. As Prole shut her office door, her staffers hurried back to their desks, completely inspired by their candidate.

Meanwhile, Daphne pushed a hank of hair from her brunette wig out of her eyes and leaned toward Carmen.

"'Hates to be the center of attention,' my butt," she whispered. "That Middie Prole is faker than my hair color. She makes me so mad!"

But when Daphne looked to Carmen for affirmation, the OSS agent was grinning from ear to ear.

"Oh, no," Daphne said. "You're not under the C-3's spell, too, are you?"

"No way," Carmen assured the star. "But I *am*

onto an opportunity. Middie Prole is alone, away from the eyes of her devoted supporters. This is our chance!"

"Fab!" Daphne said excitedly. "What can I do?"

"You can wait in the van with Charlotte while we pull a dangerous spy maneuver," Carmen instructed Daphne.

"What?" Daphne said. "But . . . but . . ."

"Daphne, you're a musician," Carmen said seriously. "Well, sorta. Anyway, I don't have to tell you about the importance of rehearsal. And we Cortezes have been practicing our martial arts maneuvers for years. We're a tight team. You can't just jump in at the last minute. It could jeopardize our whole mission."

When Daphne pouted, Carmen gave her a pointed look.

"Plus," she added, "it would be really diva-ish."

"All right, all right," Daphne said. "I hear ya. We'll be waiting in the van. With the engine running and snacks at the ready."

"Thanks," Carmen said. Then she went to join her family. They'd stolen in to the coffee room, where they were already checking out their spy gadgets and plotting away. As Carmen watched her family ponder their various gizmos, she began to get antsy. Their alone time with the candidate was melting away! They had to act!

"You know what?" Carmen finally announced. "I think we should go gadget-less. We don't have time to sift through all this stuff. And besides, who knows how *our* hardware will react with *hers*?"

Juni's eyes grew wide.

"I hadn't thought of that," he said. "The C-3 is a mystical gem. It could completely mess with our gizmos' get-up-and-go."

"So we'll battle Prole with one of our spy schemes," Carmen declared. "With our strength and cunning."

"With . . . Maneuver No. 32-B—the Spin Cycle," Dad suggested. "What do you say?"

"You got it, Dad," Carmen said.

"Okay, everybody take one of Uncle Machete's Anti-Dizziness Pills, and we'll be on our way," Mom said. She popped four tablets out of a tiny first-aid kit in her pink purse.

The spies took their medicine and snuck out of the coffee room. Then they stole into Middie Prole's office. They were so silent and stealthy the politician didn't even notice them. She was too busy poring over her press clips and cackling in vain delight.

"They love me," she whispered to herself. "They really love me! And this is just the beginning!"

"Actually, Ms. Prole," Juni piped up from behind the woman. "This is the end."

"Huh?"

Prole jumped in her seat, then twisted to look at the spies.

"*What* did you just say to me?" Prole asked Juni. She unfolded her tall body from her chair and glared down at him.

But Juni wasn't scared. In fact, he wasn't even looking at Middie Prole's face. He was eyeing her neck. Or, more specifically, the round lump hanging from a chain around her neck.

I *will* get that C-3, Juni thought with determination. And then—he began to spin!

He twirled in place so fast Prole seemed to get dizzy just looking at him! And that was exactly the effect he'd intended.

As Juni whirled, Mom began to trot in a circle, moving clockwise around the office.

And Dad started running counterclockwise.

Middie Prole got dizzier still.

Then, Carmen went in for the big finale. She began leaping into the air, doing triple axels right over Prole's head!

"Whoa!" Prole shouted.

She tried to focus on Mom. Then on Dad. Then on the swirling Spy Kids. Her left eye went right and her right eye went left and then they crossed altogether!

"She's weakening," Mom called, without breaking her stride. "Fall in, troops! One . . . two . . ."

"*Three!*" all four Cortezes shouted.

Abruptly, they quit spinning and lunged at the villain. Dad and Juni each grabbed one of Prole's hands. Mom pulled at the neck of the woman's sweater. And Carmen got to work on the clasp of the C-3's gold chain. She had just closed her fingers around the tiny ring when suddenly, she felt a jolt of electricity—in her toes!

"*Eeek!*" Carmen shrieked. She dropped the necklace and began hopping wildly around the office. She shook one foot, then the other, trying to rid her toes of the sparking.

The sensation was so awful she almost didn't notice the rest of her family going through their own strange reactions.

Mom's hair had suddenly shot straight up in a cloud of crackling static electricity. With a yelp, she took her hands off Prole's sweater and began to clutch at her own crazy curls.

Meanwhile, Juni was panting like a dog who'd just eaten a handful of chili peppers. And Dad was reaching desperately for an unreachable itch on his back!

By now, Middie Prole's googly eyes had gone back to normal. She watched the spies' struggles and laughed maniacally.

"It's like the C-3 has put out some sort of force field," Carmen screeched as she hopped around the office.

"One that attacks each of us in a different, horrible way," Juni panted. "It's not a force field. *Huh, huh, huh*. It's a *fource* field!"

"That's four fields too many!" Dad cried, scratching desperately. "Retreat, *mi familia*! Retreat!"

CHAPTER 10

Only seconds later, the Cortezes tumbled into the minivan outside the campaign headquarters. Daphne was waiting in the backseat, and Charlotte was up front, quietly knitting.

"Drive!" Dad grunted, flopping into the back of the van and clawing wildly at his back.

"Who . . . me?" the startled Charlotte quavered.

"Yes, you!" Mom screeched as she batted at her outrageous hair. "We've got to make a quick getaway. And as you can see, Charlotte, we're having a few, uh, problems."

"Problems? *Huh-huh-huh*," Juni panted. "I would say, *huh-huh-huh,* this qualifies as a fiasco!"

"Can we talk terminology later?" Carmen shrieked. She'd just torn off her sensible politician's shoes and was blowing on her sparking toes. "Right now, we just need to dash. Drive, Charlotte, drive!"

"Please!" Dad cried.

"Uh—okay," Charlotte stuttered. Sidling over to

the driver's seat, she turned the ignition key with trembling fingers. Then she lurched out of the parking lot and began to drive away. The farther the van got from the building, the fainter the spies' symptoms became. In about ten miles or so, the sparking in Carmen's toes had subsided to a mere tingling, and Dad's itching had stopped. Mom's hair began to feel normal again, and Juni was actually able to close his mouth. The spies slumped into their seats, sighing with relief.

Daphne looked to them for the scoop.

"First of all," she said. "Are you all okay? And second, did you snag the C-3?"

The Cortezes shook their heads sorrowfully in answer to the latter question and filled Daphne in on the entire botched mission. When they'd finished the story, Daphne blinked in bewilderment.

"That's weird," she said. "The C-3 never made a force field for me! Especially when I needed it most—the moment the gem was stolen!"

"If only we knew more about this mysterious Charlatan Chanteuse Crystal," Carmen complained.

"Yeah," Daphne sighed. She mulled over the situation for a despondent moment. Suddenly, she perked up.

"Hey," she said. "Maybe there's something about this in the C-3 manual!"

"The C-3 manual?" the four Cortezes shouted.

"Daphne!" Juni added. "You mean there's intel on this thing that you didn't tell us about?"

Daphne shrugged guiltily.

"It didn't occur to me until just now," she said. "I'm not what you'd call the bookish type."

"Is that so?" Mom said. She leaned into the van's front seat and stared accusingly at Charlotte, who was supposed to be, after all, Daphne's tutor.

"I'm . . . I'm sorry," Charlotte said. Her cheeks became whiter than their usual shade of pale. "But *you* try to make a willful pop star do her homework!"

"Maybe I will!" Mom said, returning to the backseat. Now she was giving Daphne a hard look. Cringing under Mom's scrutiny, Daphne tried to divert the conversation to more urgent matters.

"Listen," she said to Carmen. "The manual's on a Web site, but it's totally encrypted. If you can decipher it, maybe we can find out something important."

"*If?*" Carmen repeated. Her face got stony. "Please, Daphne. I'm a master hacker. There's no Web site I can't wrangle. Hand me that laptop!"

Daphne pulled a computer case from beneath the seat and passed it to Carmen.

"I'll type the Web address," she said. She tapped out a long series of numbers and letters. Then she passed the computer to Carmen.

"Hmmm," Carmen said, looking at the site. She began to type with great intensity.

After a few minutes, she lifted her fingers from the keyboard and announced, "Done!"

The star and the spies leaned over the computer. They skimmed over a very long, very boring history of the C-3 and a list of rules and regulations. Then they got to a section that made Juni perk up.

"'Loopholes and Quagmires,'" he said, reading the section heading aloud. "That sounds juicy. Let's see. . . . Yup, here's a paragraph all about the force field!"

"But what about the *lack* of a force field?" Daphne wondered aloud.

Carmen scrolled down the screen. Then she jumped.

"Check this out," she exclaimed. "It says here, 'The C-3's power depends on its owner's ability to keep a secret. Each time a diva tells a living soul about her jewel, the C-3's strength diminishes—in both its power to protect *and* its power to persuade.'"

"Heavy," Juni breathed. "So, clearly, Middie Prole has kept the C-3 secret."

"But so did I!" Daphne cried.

"Daphne," Mom said gently. "Whom did you tell?"

"I swear, I didn't tell a soul about the C-3," Daphne said. "Not until after it was stolen. That's when I told Carmen and Juni, and then Charlotte."

"Daphne," Dad said seriously. "You're certain of this?"

"Absolutely," Daphne said. "I didn't tell a soul."

"Which means," Juni said craftily, "maybe somebody found out without your knowledge!"

"Somebody who could keep a secret!" Carmen said.

"Somebody with constant access to you," Juni added. "An entourage member who would sell his soul—or the C-3—to Middie Prole in exchange for political power."

A look of hurt and betrayal flickered across the pop star's face.

"I can't imagine who would do that," she squeaked. "I thought my entourage . . . really cared about me."

Carmen put a sympathetic hand on Daphne's shoulder. Then she asked gently, "Where are your peeps now?"

"They went to Lear Manor," Daphne said.

"That's my mansion in Alabama. Mama said they were going to stay there until I recovered from my 'laryngitis.'"

Carmen nodded somberly. Then she leaned into the van's front seat.

"Charlotte?" she said. "Let's start driving south. It's time to see what our Learjets are up to!"

CHAPTER 11

For Juni, the next few hours were defined by snack stops. As the minivan left Washington, they pulled over for a lunch of crab cakes. Dinner in Tennessee was barbecued ribs. And breakfast the next morning, in Alabama, was grits and biscuits with sausage gravy.

Juni was almost bummed when the road trip ended a few hours later, in Frog Woods, Alabama.

As Dad drove the van down a long, tree-lined driveway, both Spy Kids stared out the window and gasped. Lear Manor was huge! Scampering about the grounds were peacocks with permanently fanned tails and dozens of tropical songbirds; there was even a cuddly koala perched high up in a magnolia tree!

But those animals were nothing compared to the mansion itself. The huge building was constructed of pink marble. It was surrounded by two swimming pools, a tennis court, and Daphne's own drive-in movie theater!

"C'mon in," Daphne said as Dad parked the car. "Make yourselves at home."

"Oh, uh, sure," Carmen stuttered, as a servant rushed to meet the spies at the door and take their bags.

"This is about as homey as a shopping mall," Juni muttered, stumbling through a high-ceilinged, sculpture-filled foyer into a huge living room. Lounging on various leather sofas were a number of Daphne's family and so-called friends.

"Daph!" Kirstie cried, running over to give Daphne a hug. "You're back from vacation! How *are* you? Did you bring any souvenirs?"

"Like Brandon Crushman, for instance?" Christie asked, as she skipped over to give the star a squeeze of her own.

"No, uh, just me," Daphne said with a shrug.

"Oh," the girls said blankly, in unison.

"Well, maybe at the next tour stop," Kirstie said cheerfully. "I assume, since your voice has returned, that you're ready to re-rev the party?"

"Um . . ."

"Daphne!" Carmen cut in, grabbing the girl by the arm. "Didn't you say you wanted to show me the mansion's underground escape passage? You know, for security reasons."

"Er, uh, yeah, I did say that, didn't I?" Daphne replied, flashing Carmen a grateful grin. The girls ducked out of the living room. As they crossed a giant kitchen—outfitted, of course, in all the latest appliances, including a giant oil drum for deep-frying Southern delicacies—Daphne gazed at Carmen in surprise.

"How did you know about the underground escape passage?" she demanded.

"Please. Every paranoid pop star's mansion has one," Carmen said, waving her hand dismissively. "I bet you have a private recording studio and a bed-room converted into a closet, too."

"And a bowling alley and a fully stocked cream-ery near the stream out back," Daphne admitted. "Man, I really did lose perspective, didn't I?"

"It could happen to anyone," Carmen said, as the girls entered a game room stuffed with six dif-ferent video game systems, a pink pool table, and a karaoke stage. Before the girls could cross the room, however, Carmen spotted something. Catching her breath, she pulled Daphne into a shadowy hiding place behind one of the video games.

In the center of the game room, a TV news camera was trained on a milky-skinned young man in hip-looking spectacles and a razor-sharp suit. Standing behind the camera, holding a microphone, was a reporter.

"That's Mickey O'Ritz, my agent from IAB," Daphne whispered to Carmen. "Looks like he's being interviewed."

"Yes, Daphne's devastated by her recent bout with laryngitis," Mickey was saying to the reporter. "That's why, when she's back on her feet, she'll return to a newly expanded concert tour!"

"What?!" Daphne gasped quietly. "We're already going to twenty-eight cities! Do you know how much work that is?"

Carmen nodded sympathetically and turned her gaze back to the interview.

"Wow," the reporter was saying. "Daphne Lear works hard for the money. I mean, that *is* why you're expanding the tour, isn't it? To recoup financial losses from this setback?"

"Oh, yes," Daphne whispered angrily.

"Oh, *no*," Mickey protested. "This isn't about my—er—*Daphne's* money. It's about the fans! Daphne would die before disappointing them."

"Hmmm," Carmen muttered. Then she led

Daphne away from the game room. Heading back to the living room, they ran into Juni, Mom, and Dad. Each had been spying on the Learjets in various parts of the mansion. While Daphne went to the kitchen for a glass of iced tea, the Cortezes quietly conferred.

"I just saw Ginny Jo ordering the entire contents of a clothing catalog," Mom reported. "It looks like Daphne's mama has really gotten used to the good life."

"Meanwhile, her little sister is meeting with one of the concert managers," Juni said. "She was asking if she could fill in while Daphne's out sick."

"And *I* just saw one of the publicists calling a book editor," Dad whispered. "She was offering to write a tell-all biography of Daphne—for the right price, that is!"

"It looks like *anyone* in this house is power-hungry enough to have stolen the C-3!" Carmen said.

"It's kinda sad, when you think about it," Juni said. "Daphne's entourage cares more about her fame and money than they do about her! They're total users!"

The Spy Kids shook their heads in sympathy for Daphne. It was only when Dad put a finger to his chin and began to muse out loud that they refocused their attention on their mission—finding out who had stolen the C-3 for Middie Prole.

"These Learjets *are* slimy," Dad admitted. "And they're definitely using poor Daphne. But that's the thing. For them to become rich and famous, they *need* Daphne. Destroying her just puts their own meal tickets at risk. So why would they steal her C-3?"

"Good point, honey," Mom said. A troubled frown furrowed her forehead. "I guess we'll just have to keep spying until we find an answer."

"Let's split up again," Juni said. "We haven't even covered the residential wing yet."

"Or the fully outfitted day spa *or* the designer chicken coop," Carmen agreed.

On that note, the spies sneaked back out of the living room. Waving good-bye to his family, Juni slunk up the stairs to the second floor.

Skulking from doorway to doorway, he peeked in on one Learjet having her hair done in the beauty room and another working out with a personal trainer in the gym.

Then Juni smelled something.

Something sweet.

And something sausagey!

"*Mmmm,*" he whispered, feeling his stomach rumble. He hadn't had anything to eat since that morning's grits break. Leaving several rooms unspied upon, Juni drifted down the long hallway to an office in the mansion's west wing.

Peeking in, he saw Nigel Knot, Daphne's hyper-organized manager. He was sitting at a desk covered with receipts, business reports, and other important papers.

Also on the desk was a plate of fragrant food. The skinny, bald-pated Nigel was hunched over the plate, devouring the grub with abandon. And, as usual, he was talking on his cell phone.

"I tell you, man," Nigel was saying in his clipped British accent. "The Yanks came to America to escape persecution, and now they turn around and persecute the Brits!"

Angrily Nigel scooped a spoonful of mashed potatoes into his mouth, then took a bite of a big sausage.

"What I'm talking about is my work visa," Nigel said into the phone. "In order to stay in the States and work for Daph, I've got to renew my visa. And the government's being right obstinate about it, they are. It's humiliating. In fact, it's *infuriating*!"

The skinny manager growled and took a big bite

of toast spread with some gloppy brown stuff. Clearly, stress made Nigel hungry. Juni could relate! He clutched his stomach and suppressed a moan as Nigel went on.

As Nigel complained, Juni began to make some clever deductions.

Of all the Learjets in this house, he realized suddenly, Nigel is the hungriest. And not just for food! He wants power, influence, and freedom!

But he's an English citizen, Juni thought, with wide eyes. He can't run for office here. He can't even vote! The only way for him to gain power in the United States is through somebody else! Somebody like . . . Middie Prole! Maybe Prole had made a deal with Nigel: if he got her the C-3, she'd reward him with megaperks once she was in the White House!

The whole scheme became crystal-clear—make that Charlatan Chanteuse Crystal–clear. Juni just had to tell his family! He was sneaking away to do just that when something Nigel said caught his ear.

He was talking about Juni's favorite subject—food!

"What's that?" Nigel said into the phone, with his mouth full. "Am I eating? Of course! I'm a busy man, especially now that I'm running interference for our little diva. Gotta multitask, I do. Besides, can you blame me? These are my favorite foods. Beans on toast and Bangers and mash!"

Beans on toast! Juni thought. Gross. And what kind of ridiculous name is Bangers and mash?!

Clearly, Nigel's phone buddy had asked the same question.

"What?" Nigel complained. "Now you're persecuting me, too? C'mon! English food is delicious!"

Juni clamped his teeth together to keep from laughing.

"The best part is dessert," Nigel said dreamily. "A Curly Wurly candy bar!"

That was it! Juni couldn't take it anymore. He let out an uncontrollable snort of laughter.

"Hang on!" Nigel exclaimed, twisting in his chair.

Juni gulped down his giggle. Uh-oh.

Nigel snapped his phone shut. Then he launched himself from his chair with a roar.

An *evil* roar.

Before Juni could run away, Nigel was lunging through the office door. And he was making a grab for Juni!

CHAPTER 12

"**W**hoa!" Juni shouted, jumping out of the way an instant before Nigel's hands closed upon his shoulders.

Juni began to run down the hallway.

"C'mere, you!" Nigel roared. Juni heard the furious Brit's big, clunky shoes clomping after him.

And he was coming fast!

Juni—who was a few feet shorter than Nigel— would never outrun him. He had to hide! And he had to hide in a spot too small for any grown-up.

Like, Juni thought desperately, that laundry chute at the end of the hall! Breaking into a sprint, he dived for the small, round door in the wall near the staircase. He began to slide down the slick, silver tunnel. Behind him, he heard Nigel Knot's frustrated shouts.

"Yay!" Juni said happily as he slid downward. "How often does a spy get to evade evil so easi— uh-oh!"

Juni's relief melted away as he focused on something up ahead: a four-way split in the laundry chute, fronted by several claw-tipped, robotic arms. And the claws did *not* look friendly.

"Oh, no!" Juni realized suddenly. "This is a *self-sorting* laundry chute! All the stars have them! I shoulda known!"

It was too late to do anything but slide into the sorting area. With a sinister grinding of gears, the metal arms began to poke and prod at Juni's clothes.

The PLEATHER/VINYL/RAYON claw passed over him quickly. After a few painful prods, the PERMANENT PRESS arm rejected him, too. STRETCH DENIMS AND OTHER UNSHRINKABLES considered Juni's slightly snug OSS uniform suspiciously. But then it, too, passed him by.

The only choice left was the dreaded DRY CLEAN ONLY chute.

"No!" Juni gasped.

But he was no match for the powerful claw. Picking him up by the collar of his high-tech shirt, the robotic arm tossed Juni into the REJECT chute.

"*Aaaaaaghhhhh!*" the Spy Kid shrieked as he tumbled downward.

"Oooooff!" he grunted as the tunnel spat him out, onto a very hard floor.

Then Juni sighed as he looked around. The laundry chute had deposited him at the base of the staircase in the dramatic-looking foyer. It was a convenient place for a servant to grab a pile of dry cleaning. And a *very* convenient place for Nigel Knot to overtake Juni. At that very moment, in fact, the villain was beginning to race down the stairs!

Juni's only choice was to plant his feet and put up his fists. So that's exactly what he did.

As he descended the stairs, Nigel's long, thin fingers closed into fists. Behind his glasses, his eyes narrowed to slits.

Meanwhile, Juni set his jaw and readied himself for a brutal fight. Only a miracle could save him now!

Whirrrrrrrrrr.

"Hey, Spy Boy!"

Juni jumped. That was Carmen's voice! As usual, his big sister was bossing him around.

"Hop on!"

Before Juni could react, something swept him off his feet. Then it swept him right out of the foyer. Literally! Juni gasped loudly as he realized that he was clinging to the base of a giant, humming vacuum cleaner! Sitting behind him—on a bouncy seat built into the air-filled dust bag—was Carmen. She was steering the vacuum cleaner with a joystick and grinning.

"Forget those tractor lawn mowers," Carmen said, shaking her head incredulously. "This is a ride-on *vacuum* cleaner! And I thought Uncle Machete's household helpers were excessive!"

"Please," Juni said, shaking his head. "The whole celebrity lifestyle thing is completely crazy! But here's something that's no joke! Nigel's our baddie!"

"I gathered," Carmen said, glancing over her shoulder. She'd just driven the vacuum cleaner through Daphne's elaborate entertainment center and steamy plant conservatory. Now she was steering the humming appliance into the gold-painted ballroom. Even using the vacuum cleaner's turbo speed setting, they hadn't completely lost Nigel. He was sprinting after the Spy Kids with a murderous leer.

"Evasion is pointless," Carmen said. "Nigel's got to know this mansion's every hiding place. But we *do* have something on the guy."

"What?" Juni asked.

"Supersucking attachments!"

With a sly smile, Carmen pulled a hose out of the base of the vacuum cleaner. At its end was a round, bristly cup. The attachment was spinning fast enough to give brush burns and sucking up so much oxygen Juni began to feel lightheaded.

"Perfect!" he breathed. "Let's get him!"

Abruptly, Carmen yanked backward on the joystick. The vacuum cleaner changed direction—and began barreling straight toward Nigel!

"I'll get you, you little troublemakers," Nigel growled, as the kids approached.

"Not, Knot!" Juni quipped. While Carmen steered the vacuum cleaner deftly around the villain, Juni grabbed the swirling brush. He plunked the attachment onto Nigel's shiny, bald head. The supersucker attached itself to the villain's scalp with a *thwack*!

"Aaaaigggh!" Nigel shouted, batting wildly at the hose. But it was hopeless. The ride-on vacuum cleaner was running on 75,000 STUs (Sucking Thermal Units). Nigel had been caught.

"The only thing that could unstick you," Juni crowed, as the manager flailed and wailed, "is some axle grease! Ha-ha-h—"

Abruptly, Juni's gloating ground to a halt. Because the moment he'd said the word "grease," Nigel's face had become sly and scheming. He reached into the pocket of his skinny black pants and pulled out a small, glass jar. He held it up so that the horrified Spy Kids could read its label: "Baldo Balm—for a supershiny scalp. The first choice of hairless celebrities everywhere!"

With a cackle, Nigel opened the jar, scooped out a big gob of Baldo Balm, and slicked it onto his head.

The swirling brush immediately slid off Nigel's head! And Juni—who was still grasping the attachment's hose—went with it!

"*Aaaaaiiigggh!*" Juni shouted as he careened through the air. He landed on the ballroom's parquet floor with a thud.

"*Urgh,*" the Spy Boy groaned. Woozily, he pulled himself to his feet. He closed his eyes until they got ungoogly.

He turned back toward the humming vacuum cleaner to see what was happening. Surely Carmen had already positioned another attachment on Nigel. In a moment, Juni would leap to her aid.

There was just one problem.

The vacuum cleaner was still parked in the

middle of the dance floor, sucking every speck of dust in the room into its powerful tube.

But Nigel—along with Carmen—had disappeared!

For a split second, Juni simply gaped at the riderless vacuum cleaner in disbelief. He began to run toward one of the ballroom doors. He had to rescue his sister!

"No, don't!"

Juni skidded to a halt. That was Carmen's voice! Juni looked around wildly. Where was his sister hiding?

"In your spy watch, dorkus!" Carmen said. Juni nodded. Of course. Carmen's voice was echoing quietly from the walkie-talkie speaker in Juni's watch.

"Where are you?" Juni demanded.

"I'm in a room somewhere in the basement," Carmen said. "There are microphones everywhere, and there's foam rubber on the walls. It must be a recording studio. Nigel dumped me in here, tied me up, and left. But not before he locked about a million bolts on the door. He said he was going to get something, and he'd be right back!"

"Okay, just hang on," Juni said. "I'm coming to the rescue."

"Like I said the first time—don't!" Carmen said irritably.

"Ex-*cuse* me?" Juni huffed. "Hello? One of us gets taken hostage, and the other one swoops in to the rescue. This is what we do."

"But *first* we focus on the mission," Carmen retorted from Juni's spy watch speaker. "We're supposed to be bodyguarding Daphne Lear. Now that Nigel knows we're onto him, she could be in danger. For all we know, he's tracking her down somewhere in Lear Manor as we speak!"

"You're right!" Juni agreed.

"I can stall Nigel," Carmen said. "You get Daphne out of there."

"Roger," Juni replied. After sending his parents a quick SOS through *their* spy watches, he dashed off in search of the pop star.

Juni raced through the endless rooms and hallways of Lear Manor. But Daphne seemed to have disappeared, too.

"Let's see," Juni muttered as he ran. "If I were a deposed diva, where would I be?"

Juni pondered Daphne Lear. He remembered her country-style sack of horehound candy. And her cross-stitch hoop. And the Southern twang in her voice.

And that was when Juni figured out where he'd find her!

To the front porch! he said to himself. Dashing through the foyer, Juni slammed out Lear Manor's front door.

Sure enough, there was Daphne Lear. She was sitting on a porch swing, stitching away between sips of iced tea. Nearby, Charlotte was curled up with a book.

"Daphne!" Juni cried, running over to the cross-stitching star. "You're in danger! You've gotta bolt."

"But where?" Daphne sputtered.

"No time to explain," said a voice behind them. Juni, Daphne, and Charlotte whirled around to see Mom hurrying onto the porch. Dad was right behind her.

"There's an OSS safe house just a few miles away from here," Mom informed Daphne, finding the address in the database on her spy watch. "You and Charlotte take the minivan and get there ASAP. Stop for no one. Speak to no one. And don't leave until we come for you. Understood?"

For once, the diva demanded no more explanations. She just nodded meekly. "I understand," she said. Then she and Charlotte hurried away.

As soon as they'd seen the minivan peel away

from Lear Manor, the three Cortezes gave one another determined looks. One part of the mission completed, one more to go.

"Now," Juni said. "Let's go find Carmen!"

CHAPTER 13

Carmen sat in the recording studio, glaring at the duct tape that bound her to her chair. She *hated* it when kidnappers tied her up with tape. She much preferred ropes. Untying knots was one of her specialties. Plus, ropes didn't leave sticky stuff all over her wrists and ankles.

Still, what choice did she have? Using her spy skills, Carmen began twisting and turning herself in her bindings. She estimated she'd be free in three minutes.

Alas, at minute number two, Nigel stomped back into the recording studio! He loomed over Carmen, baring his teeth and growling like a mad English foxhound.

But Carmen wasn't cowed. She sneered right back as she said, "Your jig is *so* up, Nigel Knot."

"Oh, I believe it's the other way around, Spy Kid," Nigel retorted. "You're going to explain yourself, right now!"

He thrust into Carmen's hands—a computer printout?!

"Uh . . . what is that?" Carmen asked, thoroughly confused.

"You tell me!" Nigel growled.

Carmen looked at the glossy, color printout. It was an article from the gossip-mongering Web site *Celeb Web*! On the top of the page was a photo of Daphne in her dark, wavy wig. The fuzzy photo—obviously taken from a great distance with a zoom lens—showed her grinning and licking some type of sauce off her finger.

"'One of our Tennessee-based paparazzi spied teen dream queen Daphne Lear feasting on barbecued ribs last night,'" Carmen read out loud. "'Her raven wig and newly sweet smile might have fooled her fans, but not us! Hey, you'd smile, too, if you'd deceived thousands of ticket-buyers into believing you'd canceled a concert on account of laryngitis. But when we heard Daphne utter, clear as a bell, the words "May I have more iced tea, please?" it seemed her raspy voice had been miraculously revitalized. As for Lear's uncharacteristic politeness, *CW* is befuddled. Could this be the end of Daphne Lear as we know her?'"

Carmen finished reading. Then she swallowed

guiltily. It was one thing to sneak around as an anonymous spy. Clearly, it was quite another when you were the star of the century. Daph's cover had been totally blown!

"Um . . . oops," Carmen said, shrugging at the manager guiltily.

Nigel tore the printout in half and began pacing angrily in front of Carmen.

"Oops, huh?" he ranted. "That isn't going to cut it, my little crumpet! Daphne's on the verge of ruin! If she doesn't sing at her next concert, I'm not sure her career will survive the bad publicity. And lemme tell you, missy, I've worked with Daphne Lear since she was twelve. She may be a pain in the, uh, crumpet, but she's also the most dedicated star I know. Singing is her life. She's worked too hard to let it fall to pieces. I won't *let* that happen to her."

Nigel leaned into Carmen's face and added, "That's why *you're* going to tell me how you manipulated Daphne into this phony laryngitis stunt!"

Carmen blinked in surprise. For someone who'd stolen Daphne's C-3 and sabotaged her star power, Nigel sounded an awful lot like a worried, caring . . . Dad!

Wait a minute, Carmen thought in bewilderment. Let me wrap my brain around thi—

Slaaaaammm!

"Freeze, Nigel Knot!"

It was Mom, Dad, and Juni! They'd found the
recording studio, picked its locks, and forced
the door open. Now they were in full rescue mode.
And they were going to start by pounding Daphne's
manager!

While Mom and Juni rushed over to Carmen
and began ripping away her duct tape bindings,
Dad stalked over to the now-quaking Nigel.

"Kidnapping a young girl," Dad growled. "Even
if she is an international superspy who would have
trounced you in the end—that's a despicable thing
to do."

Dad reached for the handcuffs hanging from
his utility belt.

"Maybe a few years in jail will convince you to
change your ways," he said.

"No, Dad!" Carmen cried. "Stop! Nigel's innocent."

"Huh?" Dad, Mom, and Juni—and Nigel, for
that matter—cried out.

"Innocent of what?!" Nigel sputtered.

"We'll explain on the way," Carmen said, pulling

off her last bit of duct tape and hopping out of her chair. "Let's just say, if *you*'re not our baddie, then someone else is! We need to find Daphne and make sure she's okay!"

With that, the four spies and Nigel dashed out of the basement. As they ran to Lear Manor's front door, Dad shouted, "Charlotte and Daphne took the minivan. We need wheels!"

"We'll take my car," Nigel cried. "Follow me!"

A moment later, the crew skidded to a halt in front of Nigel's car. It was the smallest, squashiest car any of the spies had ever seen! Mom and Dad rolled their eyes. Carmen stifled a giggle, but Juni couldn't contain his guffaws.

"It's like the stretch Hummer had puppies," he chortled. "And *this* is the runt of the litter!"

"What?" Nigel said defensively. "It's a mini. Very European."

Painfully, Mom, Carmen, and Juni squeezed into the backseat.

"*Ow,*" Carmen yelled as Nigel whisked them away from Lear Manor. "Juni, your knee's in my rib cage."

"That's only because Mom's elbow's knocking into my knee," Juni shot back.

"*Sommm mmmnnfftt,*" Mom replied. Her words

were muffled by Carmen's left leg, which was angled awkwardly over her face, blocking her mouth.

Luckily, the OSS safe house—an unobtrusive cottage in the woods—was nearby. Following Dad's directions, Nigel got them there in minutes. With great sighs of relief, the spies spilled out of the tiny car and bounded up the cottage steps.

Normally, this would have been the part where they burst into the house dramatically to save the day. But they didn't get that far. Because on the top step, they spotted a piece of paper. With a sinking feeling, Carmen scooped the paper up.

It was a piece of lavender stationery.

It was scented with fruity Daffy perfume.

And scrawled on the paper in pink ink was a single word: "Help!"

"Charlotte's got Daphne!" Carmen wailed, showing the note to her family. "*She*'s the saboteur."

"Mousy little Charlotte?" Nigel gasped.

"Wow, who'da thunk?" Juni said.

"Whatever," Carmen said. "Now, we've got a hostage situation. And there's only one place Charlotte could be taking Daphne."

"To Middie Prole!" Juni said. "Now that Daphne

knows Prole's secret, the evil politician is going to have to keep her quiet."

"As if ending her singing career wasn't enough," Carmen said, shaking her head sorrowfully.

As she saw dark despair begin to cloud her daughter's face, Mom broke in with a perky pep talk.

"Okay, troops," she said. "We may be down, but we are *not* out. We are *going* to rescue our rock star *and* snatch back the C-3. Are you up for it?"

Catching Mom's wave of optimism, the Spy Kids felt their enthusiasm return. "Yes!"they cried.

"You bet, honey," Dad added, giving Mom's hand a proud squeeze. Mom responded with a flirty batting of her eyelashes.

"Uh, Mom, Dad," Juni said. He planted his fists on his hips. "Could we *please* get through one mission without you two getting all mushy on us?"

"Er, sorry," Dad harrumphed, dropping Mom's hand regretfully.

"And could you *please* hit the road already?" Nigel piped up. "You have to save Daphne at all costs. And believe me, the costs are going to be high. After I cancel Daph's concert tonight, her career will be shredded. It'll all be over."

The spies went somber again. Then Juni's face

lit up. He'd just come up with a scheme—the *perfect* scheme for his sister! It was bold. It was daring. And it was definitely crazy—but it just might work, he thought.

Shooting Carmen a sly glance, Juni said to Nigel, "All over? I don't think so!"

CHAPTER 14

Carmen couldn't believe what was happening to her. She was a master hacker and a triple black belt in karate. In all her days as an international super-spy, there'd been no trap she hadn't been able to escape, no problem she hadn't been able to unravel.

Until now.

Now, she was enduring a torture unlike any she'd ever experienced.

"Okay, we're going to go over this one more time, understand?" Nigel barked.

Carmen merely gave the Brit a weary, stony glare. Ignoring her, Nigel shouted, "And a-one, and a-two, and a-one-two-three!"

Then Nigel began to roll his shiny, white head from side to side. He waggled his hips and wiggled his knees. He leaped high into the air. When he landed, his fingers were splayed. He had framed his face with the perfect "jazz hands."

When the music ended, Nigel jumped to his feet and mopped off his forehead. Then, with his arms crossed over his chest, he leaned against a wall of the mirrored Lear Manor rehearsal studio and gazed at an embarrassed Carmen.

"Your turn!" he commanded.

With a sigh and a huge roll of the eyes, Carmen began waggling her hips and wiggling her knees.

Torture, indeed, she thought wearily. Give me thumbscrews over this any day!

Mom parked the long, sleek limousine and adjusted her black chauffeur's cap.

"Well," she said, peeking out of the limo's tinted window. "We're here! A train station in East Lemming, Indiana—the heart of Middle America."

"It's also," Dad added from the backseat, where he was sitting next to Juni, "the first appearance on Middie Prole's whistle-stop campaign tour! The stage is set!"

"Is everybody in character?" Mom said, turning in the front seat to eye her son and husband. "Let's go over it one more time, okay?"

"Of course, my darling," Dad said. "A spy can never rehearse his cover too much. So allow me to introduce myself. . . ."

Reaching into the breast pocket of the sleek, dark suit he was wearing, Dad whipped out a couple of business cards. He handed one each to Mom and Juni. Then he tweaked his pencil-thin mustache proudly.

"I am Hector Machismo," he announced. "Rich. Powerful. CEO of the hot, new company Grove Computers."

"And you are?" Dad asked Juni with a gleam in his dark eyes.

"R. W. Pineapple," Juni said, raising the camera that hung around his neck to snap Dad's picture. "Reporter and photographer for the *New Amsterdam Picayune*. Nothing gets between me and a scoop, see? Nothing!"

Juni emphasized his point by taking a chomp out of his cigar—his bubble-gum cigar, that is.

"Yum!" Juni said, blowing a big bubble.

"Uh, honey," Mom said. "I can't picture a news reporter blowing bubbles and saying, 'Yum!'"

"Fair enough," Juni said, getting rid of his wad of gum. "But if we're going to stay in character, then you're not my mom. You're Hilda, the faithful chauffeur of Mr. Hector Machismo."

"Fair enough!" Mom replied with a laugh.

Chugga-chugga-chugga-CHOO-CHOOO.

The spies jumped and peered out of the limo's windows again.

"That's Middie Prole's train!" Mom announced. "It's showtime! Places, everyone!"

Carmen sat in a tall chair and tried to keep track of all the people swirling around her—a task made impossible when one of them thrust her face right into the Spy Girl's.

"Zee skeen is sallow," this woman pronounced in a haughty French accent. "Zee eyes, too brown. Zee 'air desperately needs a trim. And zee eyebrows? Don't even get me started."

The woman began smearing Carmen's face with floral-scented lotions and potions. Then she pulled out a giant sheaf of makeup brushes and began dabbing Carmen's eyes and cheeks with experimental color combos.

"You think *you've* got problems," cried a man with a long, gauzy scarf knotted around his neck. He had a dozen fabric swatches slung over his forearm and a pencil behind each ear. "She's also three sizes too small! I'm going to have to whip up fourteen *brand-new* outfits!"

The man ran to a sewing machine in the corner of the room and began frantically feeding fabric into the contraption.

Meanwhile, Nigel was busy with a cell phone

clamped to each of his ears. He was speaking so fast his lips were a blur.

And Carmen's panic was growing by the minute.

I've got to talk to Nigel, she muttered to herself. I'm starting to feel like this scheme is completely doomed!

As politely as she could, she squirmed out from under the makeup lady's flying powder brushes. She stood up and squared her shoulders.

I'm a spy, Carmen thought. If I can negotiate peace treaties with presidents and talk sense into dudes out to ruin the world, I can certainly speak my mind to a music manager!

With a brusque shake of her head, Carmen began to stalk over to Nigel.

She made it about three feet.

"Whooooaaaaa!" Carmen shrieked. She found herself careening toward the floor from what seemed a tremendous height!

The bustle in the room ground to a halt. The designer looked up from his sewing machine with a look of extreme impatience. The makeup artist curled her perfectly glossed lip. Even Nigel stopped his yammering to gaze down at Carmen and shake his head. Then he returned to his conversation.

"Sorry," he said to the person on the other end of the line. "Looks like *somebody* needs to practice walking in six-inch platform shoes!"

Carmen glanced down at her feet. She was indeed wearing towering orange patent-leather pumps! Some assistant had slipped them onto her feet when she wasn't looking!

"This is *so* humiliating," Carmen muttered to herself.

As she struggled to her feet, Nigel said into one of his cell phones, "Hang on, would ya, bloke?"

He gazed down at Carmen.

"Were you coming over—or attempting to, anyway—for any particular reason?" he asked her.

"Oh!" Carmen said, struggling to find her balance. She looked at Nigel's tired, pale face. And at the designer, who was intently sewing once again. And at the bevy of assistants scurrying through the room, talking on cell phones of their own.

Then she sighed heavily.

"No, Nigel," she said. "No, I don't have anything to say, after all."

Mom—er, that is, Hilda—led Middie Prole over to the sleek, black limousine.

"I'm sure Mr. Machismo will be very grateful

that you agreed to see him, Ms. Prole," Mom said to the candidate.

"Well, I'm always happy to meet with my voters!" Middie Prole brayed in reply. Under her breath she added, "Especially filthy-rich ones who might want to make a campaign contribution!"

Mom's OSS-honed spy skills, of course, helped her hear every word the devious Ms. Prole had just said.

As Prole got herself into the car, Mom winked at Dad—er, that is, Hector Machismo. He was seated, alone, in the backseat, with an arrogant, man-of-power expression upon his face. Once Prole was settled into the car, Mom took her seat behind the wheel.

"Ms. Prole," Dad said. "Thank you so much for seeing me on such short notice. I know you are a very busy woman."

"And you're a busy man," Prole replied. "I've heard great things about Grove Computers. You've got *quite* the up-and-coming company."

"*Sí, sí,*" Dad said, twirling his fake mustache and smiling broadly. "It is quite a task, running for president, no?" he went on, with a sly gleam in his eyes.

Prole returned the sly look. "*Sí*, it is!" she replied.

"I need to get people out to vote for me so that I can run the country."

"You know . . ." Dad continued, examining his fingernails with faux casualness. "I could . . . help you with those votes. I'm a very influential man. And a very rich one!"

"Mr. Machismo!" Prole protested in mock shock. "I do hope you're not talking about using your money and influence to buy me thousands of votes. Why, that would be wrong! Delightfully—er, I mean, *very* wrong!"

"It would *also* be our own little secret," Dad said, waggling his eyebrows at Prole.

Middie Prole's eyes narrowed.

"All right, I get it," she said. "You scratch my back, I scratch yours. So tell me, Machismo, what is it that you want?"

Dad leaned closer to Middie Prole. He grinned.

"I want nothing," he said. "Except the answer to one simple question. What is the secret of your success?"

Carmen was locked in a small storage room, deep in the basement of Lear Manor. She was hunched over a worktable, her face scrunched up in intense concentration. She'd been attending to this secret project on and off all day long. It had been tedious work.

But now . . . she was almost done.

She consulted a photograph. Then she picked up an airbrush pen and muttered, "Just a few freckles on the nose, and it'll be perfect."

Pfffftttt!

Carmen sprayed her work with a subtle smattering of pale brown. Then she tossed down her pen, dusted off her hands and announced, "*Finito!* Now, let's try it out."

She picked up her project—a rubbery, latex mask—and fitted it over her face. With only a few tugs and pulls, it was in place.

"Yes!" Carmen cried, pumping her fist. "Now I just need to find a mirror—"

Slam!

"Hey!" Carmen yelled, jumping up from her worktable. She found herself staring at a startled assistant. The young woman was holding a key to the storage room.

"Miss Lear!" the assistant cried. "I'm sorry to disturb you in here. I was just coming to get some supplies for tonight's concert. Congratulations on licking that laryngitis, by the way. The fans are gonna be so psyched to see you back in the game!"

"Oh . . ." Carmen answered. She felt a little short of breath. Had she really pulled this off?

"I mean," Carmen said quickly, remembering to speak with a Southern accent, "thanks, hon! Do you happen to have a mirror on you?"

"Sure!" the assistant said, pulling a compact out of her back pocket. "Here ya go, Miss Lear!"

Carmen opened the compact and stared at herself. But it wasn't herself blinking back at her. It was Daphne Lear, right down to the blue eyes and the freckles on the nose! The latex Daph mask Carmen had constructed was perfect!

Which meant—Carmen realized with a mixture of elation and sheer terror—that this plan was really going to work. In just a short while, she'd be impersonating Daphne Lear. Which meant, singing in front of thousands of screaming fans!

"My secret?" Middie Prole stuttered. "Mr. Machismo, whatever do you mean?"

"Please, Ms. Prole," Dad said, leaning on an armrest in the backseat of his limo. "We are both sophisticated people. And when I say sophisticated, I mean, of course, sly and devious."

"But, of course," Prole replied.

"So, I will tell you my plan," Dad said. "You tell

me your secret. I help you win this election. And someday—after you've served your two terms as president, of course—I will run for president myself. Armed with your wisdom, I will win!"

Dad watched Middie Prole's angular face go thoughtful. He could practically hear her thoughts: *Hector Machismo buys me the election. And he becomes my political successor. It's a win-win deal. I'll take it!*

Middie Prole leaned in closer.

"The secret," she confided gleefully, "is in this little thing I like to call . . . the C-3!"

Then Middie Prole launched into her story. She told Dad that she'd hired a mousy tutor to swipe the gem off some bratty pop star. She bragged about the moment she'd hung the C-3 around her own neck. Instantly, she'd had every politico in town under her spell.

In short, she spilled her guts.

Then she held her hand out to Dad.

"So, I've kept my end of the deal," she said. "Now, I'll expect you to deliver those votes! Shall we shake on it, Mr. Machismo?"

Before Dad could answer, the back door of the limousine flew open. The car was filled with a blinding flash!

"Say 'Cheese'!" said a voice. It was Juni—er, that is, R. W. Pineapple. He was poking his camera into the limo and clicking away.

"*Aaaaigggh!*" Prole cried. "What are you doing here, little boy?"

"Little boy!?" Juni sputtered. "I'm a grown man. A very—er—short grown man, named R. W. Pineapple! Pleased to meet you, Ms. Prole. Now tell me, is 'Prole' spelled with one L or two?"

Juni whipped a reporter's notebook out of his pocket and pulled a pen from behind his ear.

"You're not . . ." Prole gasped. "You can't be . . ."

"A reporter?" Juni said. "Yup! And I'm a darned good one. Listen!"

Juni reached into a corner of the limo and scooped up something that looked like a baby garter snake. He slipped the snake into his pocket. Then he pushed a button on his spy watch. Middie Prole's voice echoed through the limo.

"And now, I'll expect you to deliver those votes," she said on Juni's recording.

"What?" Prole sputtered. "But . . . how? But . . . NO!"

"Actually, yes," Juni declared as his parents looked on proudly. "I caught you buying votes. Gee, that would be pretty scandalous if I printed it in my newspaper. Some might say it could be, oh, a complete career-ender."

"Please, please don't write that story!" Prole begged. Tears began to run down her cheeks, trailing rivulets of black mascara. "I'll do anything!"

"Okay!" Juni said, snapping his notebook closed and popping a lens cap onto his camera. "Tell us where we can find Daphne Lear and Charlotte Bronstein!"

"I'll do better than that," Prole blubbered. "I'll take you to them!"

CHAPTER 15

Middie Prole lurched out of the limo with Mom, Dad, and Juni at her heels. Slipping on sunglasses and a trench coat to evade her enthusiastic political aides, Prole quickly led the spies to the train's caboose. She unlocked a gigantic padlock on the train car's door and ushered the spies inside. Huddled on the floor were the pop star and her tutor—bound and gagged!

"Daph!" Juni cried. "Charlotte! Are you all right?"

The spies leaped upon the captives, untying them in a matter of seconds.

"Thanks!" Daphne said as she spat out the handkerchief Prole had tied around her mouth. "We're okay. Especially now that you're here!"

"Yes," Charlotte said tremblingly. "I do hope you'll put that nasty woman under arrest."

"But, Charlotte," Juni blurted out in confusion. "You helped Middie with her evil scheme. *You* stole the C-3 from Daphne."

"I was just trying to teach Daphne a lesson," Charlotte protested. "Middie Prole deceived me, too! She came to me pretending to be a fellow teacher. When I told her what a horrid student Daphne was, Prole told me about the C-3. She suggested I take it away from Daphne, to teach her to stand on her own two feet. I didn't know that she just wanted the jewel for her own evil purposes. Daphne! I'm sorry!"

Daphne nodded and took Charlotte's hand.

"I *was* horrid," she admitted. "I completely understand."

"Actually, you don't," said Middie Prole from behind the group. The group turned to face the evil politician. She'd loosened the collar of her high-necked blouse so that the glinting, red C-3 was visible at her throat. Her masklike face had contorted itself into an evil scowl.

"Or you *won't* understand," she added. "Not once I get through with you. Daphne, darlin', you might not be a good student. But *I* am. In fact, I'd like to show you a little somethin' I learned from the C-3 manual!"

Then she clasped the red crystal in one hand and pointed the other hand at the group. She began to chant.

"Charlatan Crystal of the Chanteuse," she said. "Fix it so they never knew about you! Wipe all memory from their . . ."

As Prole prattled on, Juni rolled his eyes and leaned over to his mom.

"Bad poetry!" he complained. "Doesn't it seem like we get some of this on every darned mission lately? What do you think this is all about?"

"Hmmm, 'Wipe all memory from their brains,'" Mom repeated. "That sounds really familiar. . . ."

Suddenly she jumped.

"That's not poetry!" she whispered to her son. "That's an incantation! It was in the manual. Anyone who hears it forgets everything about the C-3."

"Weird," Juni said, glancing at Prole. She looked as though she were nearing the end of her chant. "But to tell you the truth, I can't say I'll be sorry to forget about that silly old necklace. It's nothing but trouble!"

"Don't be so hasty, Juni!" Mom said. Alarm was beginning to fill her green eyes. "That's a dangerous spell. The manual said there's a chance that it could wipe *all* the knowledge from our heads."

"What!?" Juni cried.

The spies exchanged a look of horror. Then they looked at Middie Prole.

"Noooooo!" Juni yelled, beginning to run toward the politician. "Stop!"

But he was too late! Before he could reach her, Prole uttered the last word of her incantation. Juni skidded to a halt and squeezed his eyes shut, prepared for all memories, all spy skills, even his own phone number to fly out of his head.

A moment later, he was still standing. And, it seemed, he was still thinking! He could remember his locker combination at school: thirty-three, eighteen, fifty-four. And he remembered his last birthday party—a trip to an amusement park and all the pizza he could eat.

And how many pizza slices was that? Juni thought. Five, that's how many! *Mmmm*, I can still taste the pepperoni.

But that means, Juni realized suddenly, that Prole's spell didn't work!

Stunned, Juni opened his eyes. Then he gasped.

His parents were standing behind the big-boned baddie. Mom was cuffing Prole's wrists behind her back, and Dad was dangling the C-3 from his fingertips! As it swung on the end of its gold chain, the crystal glinted beguilingly in the afternoon sun.

"I don't understand!" Juni sputtered. "How did you get past the force field to get the C-3?"

"I remembered a thing or two from the manual, too!" Dad announced. "Like that bit about keeping the C-3's secret, lest it lose its power. And if you remember—when Prole told me about the C-3, your mother was listening in the front seat, *and* your Eve's-Dropper was broadcasting the tale to you! That's a lot of secret-spilling!"

"And *that*'s a mission accomplished," Juni crowed. He stalked over to glare at Middie Prole. She stared down at him.

"I don't need that C-3 anymore anyway," she declared. "I've got a huge following now. The voters love me! I'm White House–bound, baby. And the first thing I'm going to do once I'm there is sign a law ousting every annoying little reporter from Washington, D.C. Maybe even the world!"

"Uh, Ms. Prole," Juni said with a smug smile. "Now that we're airing your little secrets, we've got some for you. I'm not with the *New Amsterdam Picayune.* My dad here is not Hector Machismo. And my mom may drive in the occasional car pool, but she's no chauffeur. We're all agents with the OSS! And you're under arrest!"

While Middie Prole howled in helpless outrage, Juni walked over to Dad. He took the glimmering C-3 from his father's hand.

"A deal's a deal," he said. "And Carmen and I agreed to return this stone to Daphne."

Juni handed the necklace to the pop star. Casting her eyes downward, she thanked him quietly. Then she added, "Do you happen to have a hammer on that utility belt of yours, Juni?"

"Uh . . . sure. Here's one," Juni said, pulling the rod-shaped Shift-a-Tool off his belt. He pressed a tiny button on the gizmo. With a squelching pop, the rod turned into a hammer. He handed it to Daphne. "It's an Uncle Machete classic. But what do you need a hammer for?"

"For this!" Daphne said. She dropped to her knees and placed the C-3 on the floor before her. Then she smashed it to smithereens!

"Whoa!" Juni cried. "Dramatic move, Daph!"

"I think my little gem has caused enough trouble," Daphne said. "I want nothing more to do with it."

"I'm proud of you, Daphne," Charlotte said, putting an arm around her student's shoulders. "Maybe you *have* learned a little something after all!"

Daphne's laugh sounded so much like tinkling music that Juni smiled.

"Hey," he exclaimed. "It's only two o'clock! If we

boogie, I bet we could make it to Tuscaloosa by eight."

"What's at eight?" Daphne asked innocently.

"A concert," Juni said, rubbing his hands together. "And I'm *sure* we can get backstage passes!"

Carmen Cortez sat in Daphne Lear's dressing room—hyperventilating. A gentle tap on the door startled her.

"Ten minutes to showtime, Miss Lear," a voice said.

"Thanks," Carmen squeaked.

She looked into the vanity mirror. Daphne's pretty face stared back at her, but the expression of terror was all Carmen's own.

"C'mon," she muttered to herself. "Pull yourself together. You got Daphne into this fix—now you're going to get her out of it. After all, how hard can it be to sing and dance for two hours straight . . . in front of thousands of people . . . who think I'm a gigantic star?"

Beneath her Daphne mask, Carmen felt her face go pale.

"*Aaaighh,*" she cried. "What am I doing here? Mommy!"

"Yes, sweetie?"

"Huh?" Carmen shrieked. She popped out of her chair and spun around. Her mother was at the dressing-room door, smiling reassuringly. Behind her were Dad, Juni, Daphne, Charlotte, Ginny Jo, and Nigel. They all gasped at Carmen's uncanny Daphne mask.

"You're here!" Carmen cried. "So, that means—"

"Mission accomplished," Juni announced. He quickly filled his sister in on all the details, including Daphne's smashing the C-3.

"Good for you, Daph," Carmen said, flashing the pop star a thumbs-up.

"Thanks," Daphne said. But she didn't look very happy. In fact, as she took in Carmen's rock-star makeup and concert-ready costume, she looked downright wistful.

It was a look that was not lost on the Spy Girl.

That does it, Carmen thought with relief. I'm a spy, not a star. It's time to pass the mike back to its rightful owner.

Carmen took a deep breath and pulled the Daphne mask off her face.

"What are you doing?" Daphne gasped. "You go on in five minutes!"

"No, *you* do!" Carmen said. "And you're gonna knock 'em dead."

"But you heard me sing," Daphne protested. "I was awful."

"Or maybe . . ." Carmen said thoughtfully, "you were just singing the wrong song."

She pointed at the purse slung over Daphne's shoulder.

"What's in there?" she asked. "A cross-stitch hoop and some horehound candy, right?"

"And a copy of *Gone With the Wind*," Daphne admitted.

"So maybe you should try singing what *you* like," Carmen suggested. "Instead of what you think the audience wants to hear. They might surprise you."

Daphne looked questioningly at Nigel. He bit his lip for a moment. Then he nodded at Daphne.

"Go for it, girl!" he said.

Ginny Jo stepped forward and added quietly, "Darlin'? I have some song ideas. . . . I just hope you can remember them."

Carmen saw Daphne and Ginny Jo gaze at each other across the crowded dressing room. Carmen recognized that look. It was a big mother-daughter bonding moment, one that was clearly long overdue.

When it was over, Daphne grinned and began jumping up and down in excitement.

"I'll do it!" she burbled to the rest of the group. "But first y'all have got to get out of here. I need to change!"

Ten minutes later, the Cortezes were sitting in the front row of the giant concert arena. All around them, die-hard fans were chanting, "Daphne! Daphne! Daphne!"

Carmen felt butterflies flitting around in her stomach.

"I don't know what's worse," she said to her family. "Preparing to go onstage myself, before, or waiting now to see how Daphne will pull this off!"

"I have a feeling Daphne's going to surprise us," Mom said with a grin.

Suddenly, the fans around them began screaming and stamping their feet. Daphne was striding across the stage! Instead of one of her usual sequined, skintight outfits, she was wearing a denim skirt and a pretty, white blouse. She was carrying an acoustic guitar and a tall stool. When she reached center stage, she sat down and smiled at the audience.

"I know y'all are ready to hear 'Ooey, Gooey Me,'" she said into her microphone.

The audience roared with approval.

"But I'm going to try something a little different tonight," Daphne countered. "This is a lullaby my mama used to sing to me when I was a baby. Back when we were just humble folk in Frog Woods, Alabama. I hope y'all like it."

Daphne strummed her guitar gently and began to sing. The lullaby's lyrics were happy, and the pop star's voice was as sweet as sugar! After a moment of stunned silence, the audience began to snap its fingers.

Then they all started humming along with Daphne.

By the lullaby's end, they were clapping and hooting with joy. Carmen could see Daphne flush with surprise. When she'd sung the last note, she proposed, "How about another one like that?"

"Yeah!" the crowd replied in unison.

So, for the rest of the evening, Daphne sang country melodies, Appalachian tunes, and home-spun hymns. When she bounded offstage after her final encore, the Spy Kids were there to give big congratulatory hugs!

"You were awesome!" Carmen declared. "And pretty brave, too."

"Thanks!" Daphne said. "That was the most fun I've ever had on stage! Now I guess we'll see what the critics have to say in tomorrow's papers. They don't like change very much, y'know."

"So . . . what'll you do if they don't like the new Daphne?" Carmen inquired carefully. "Will that be the end of your brief country music career?"

Daphne shrugged and grinned.

"Hey, if it is," she said, "I'll find something else to do. Like . . . spying! Your jobs are as cool as any rock gig. Maybe there's an opening at the OSS!"